SHHHHH HHHHH!

AN UGLYDOLL COMIC

KIM | HORVATH | NICHOLS | JACOBSON | MCGINTY | CHANMEN | FOWLER | SPOONS

SHHHHHHHH!
An Uglydoll Comic

Cover Art: Sun-Min Kim and David Horvath
Cover and Book Design: Fawn Lau
Editor: Traci N. Todd

Printed in China

Published by VIZ Media, LLC
P.O. Box 77010
San Francisco, CA 94107

10 9 8 7 6 5 4 3 2 1
First printing, October 2013

PARENTAL ADVISORY
UGLYDOLL: SHHHHHHHH!
is rated A and is suitable
for readers of all ages.
ratings.viz.com

WWW.VIZKIDS.COM   www.viz.com

Inside covers by Sun-Min Kim and David Horvath | **"Contagious"** story by Travis Nichols, art by Ian McGinty, colors by Michael E. Wiggam | **"So, You Want to Be a Ninja"** story by Travis Nichols, art by Ian McGinty, colors by Michael E. Wiggam | **"Frostbite"** part 1 story Travis Nichols art by Ian McGinty, colors by Michael E. Wiggam | **"Gotcha-Gotcha"** story and art by Chanmen | **"Secret Crush"** story by Travis Nichols, art by Ian McGinty, colors by Michael E. Wiggam | **"Shh! Shh!"** Story by Travis Nichols, art by Phillip Jacobson, colors by Michael Wiggam | **"Ahem!"** story by Travis Nichols, art by Phillip Jacobson, colors by Michael E. Wiggam | **"Frostbite"** part 2 Story by Travis Nichols, art by Ian McGinty, colors by Michael E. Wiggam | **"Olly, Olly Ox & Free!"** story by Travis Nichols, art by Ian McGinty, colors by Michael Wiggam | **"Outer Self Industries"** story by Travis Nichols, art by Phillip Jacobson, colors by Michael E. Wiggam | **"Shhh!"** story and art by Peter Fowler | **"Unspoken"** story by Travis Nichols, art by Phillip Jacobson, colors by Michael E. Wiggam | **"Frostbite"** part 3 story by Travis Nichols, art by Ian McGinty, colors by Michael E. Wiggam | **"Good Morning!"** story and art by Bwana Spoons | **"This Bird's Life"** story by Travis Nichols, art by Ian McGinty, colors by Michael E. Wiggam

TABLE OF CONTENTS

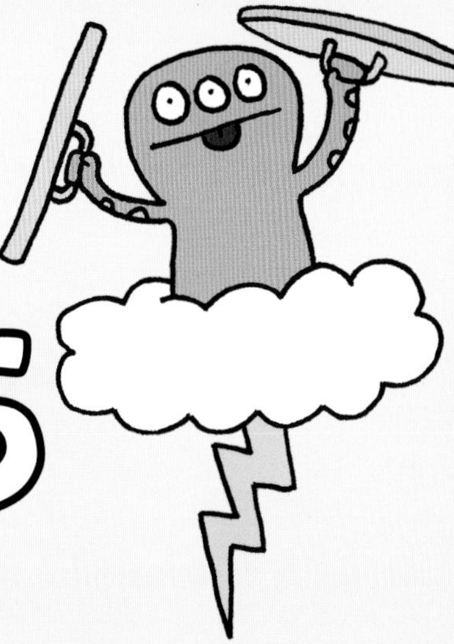

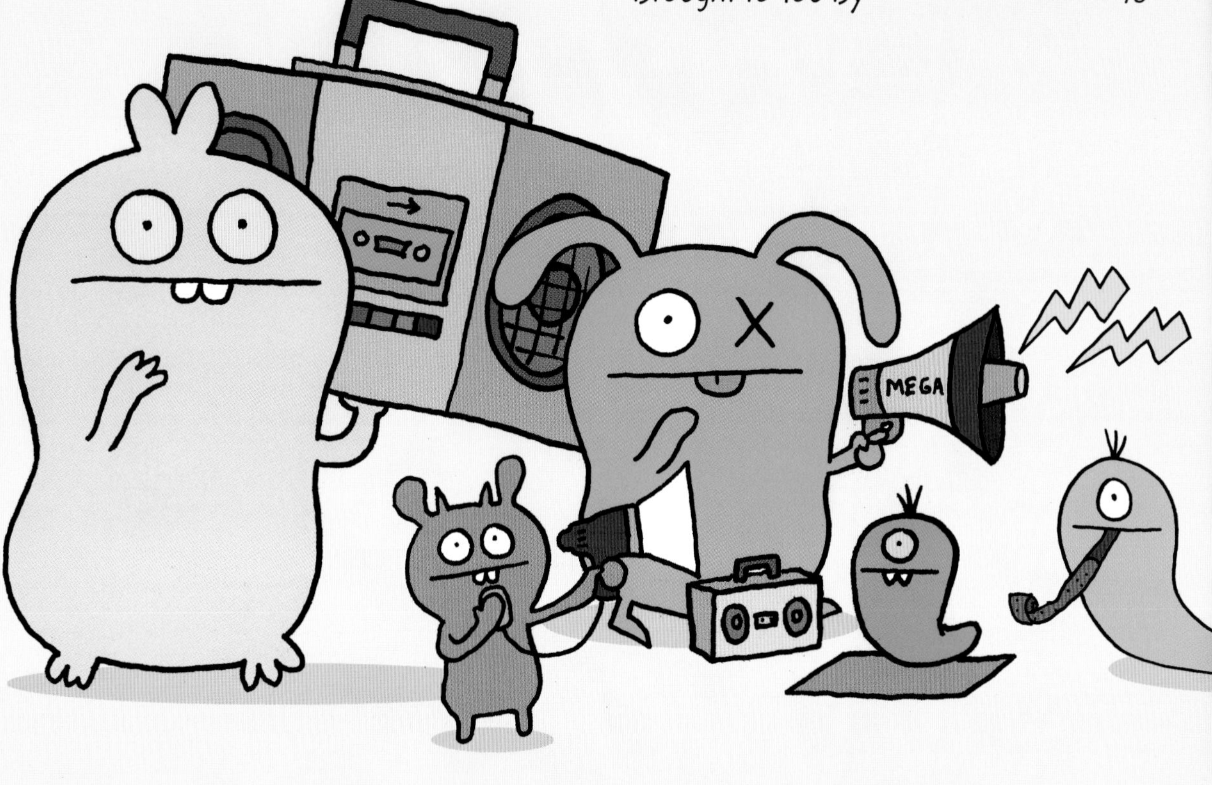

MEGA

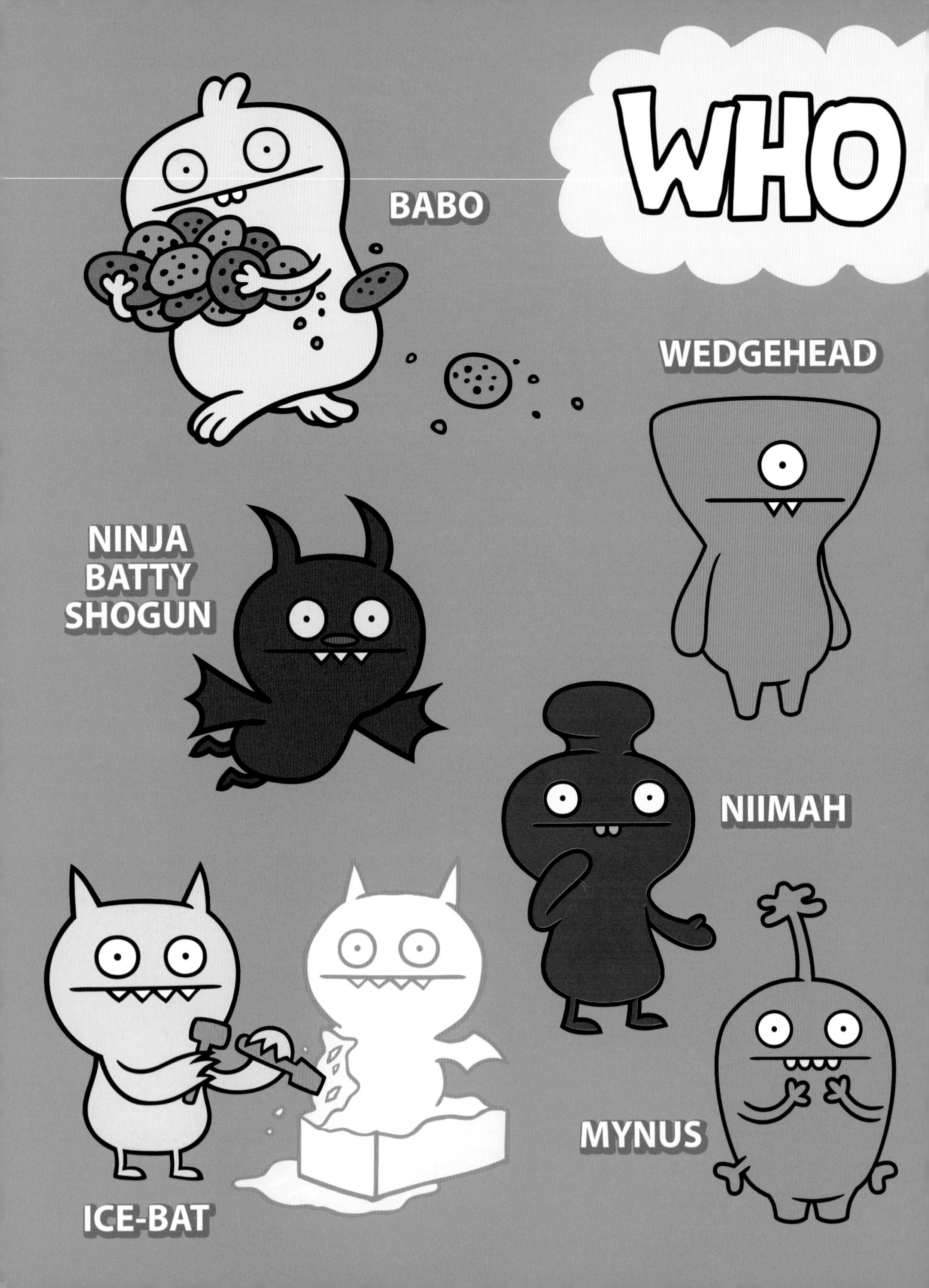
WHO
BABO
WEDGEHEAD
NINJA BATTY SHOGUN
NIIMAH
MYNUS
ICE-BAT

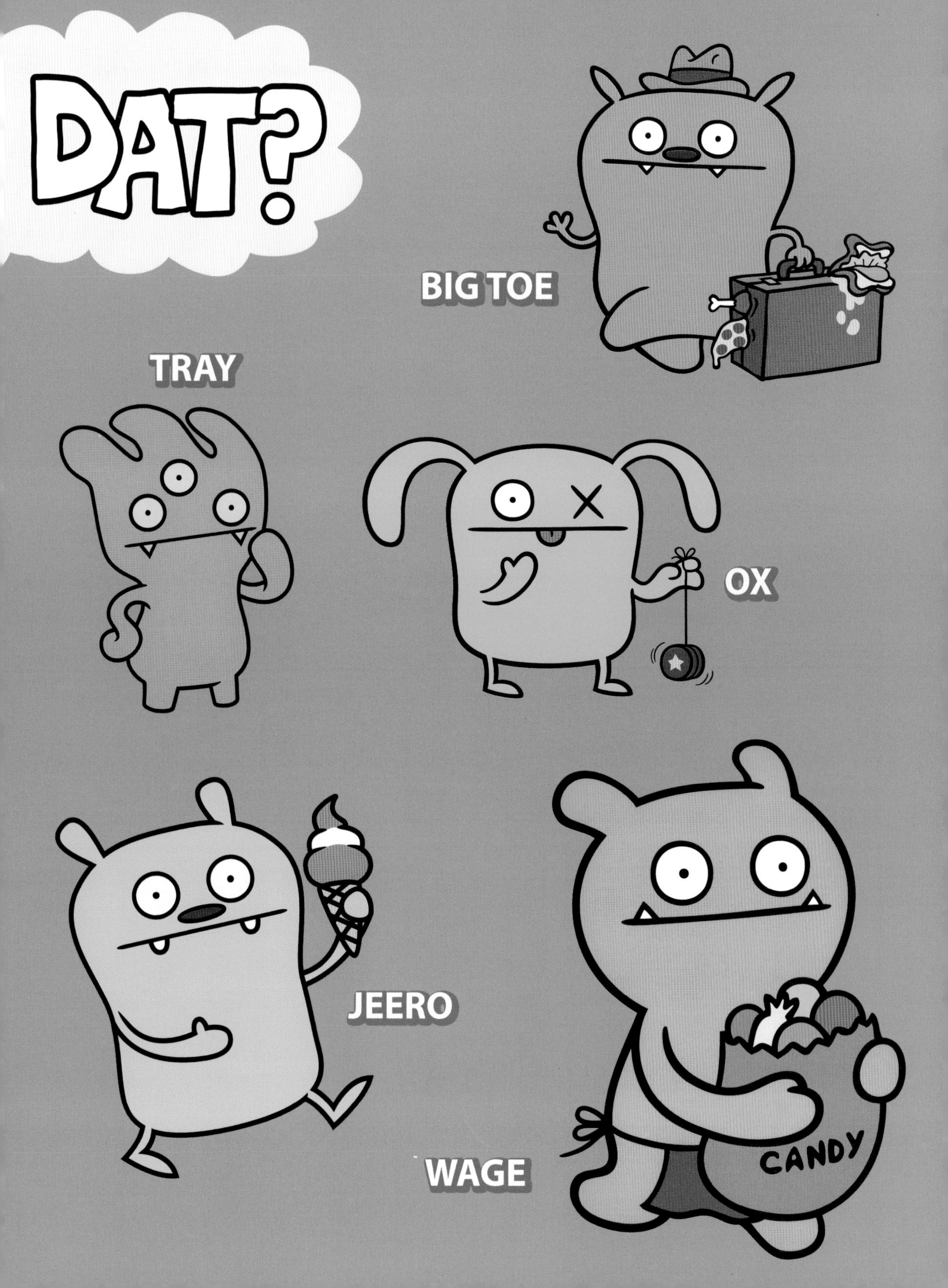
DAT?
BIG TOE
TRAY
OX
JEERO
CANDY
WAGE

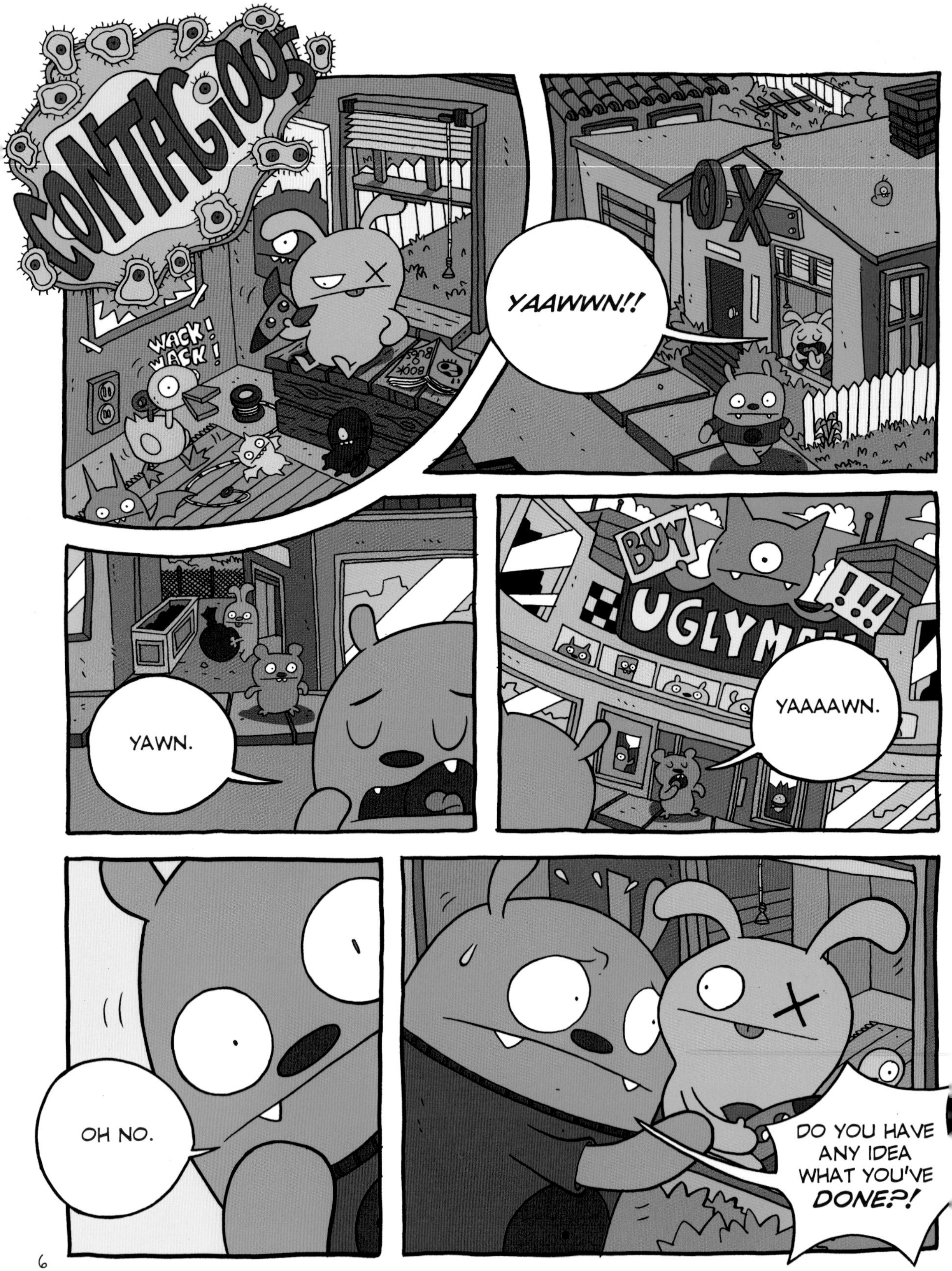
CONTAGIOUS
WACK! WACK!
BOOK O' BUGS
YAAWWN!!
OX
YAWN.
BUY
!!!
UGLYMA
YAAAAWN.
OH NO.
DO YOU HAVE ANY IDEA WHAT YOU'VE *DONE?!*

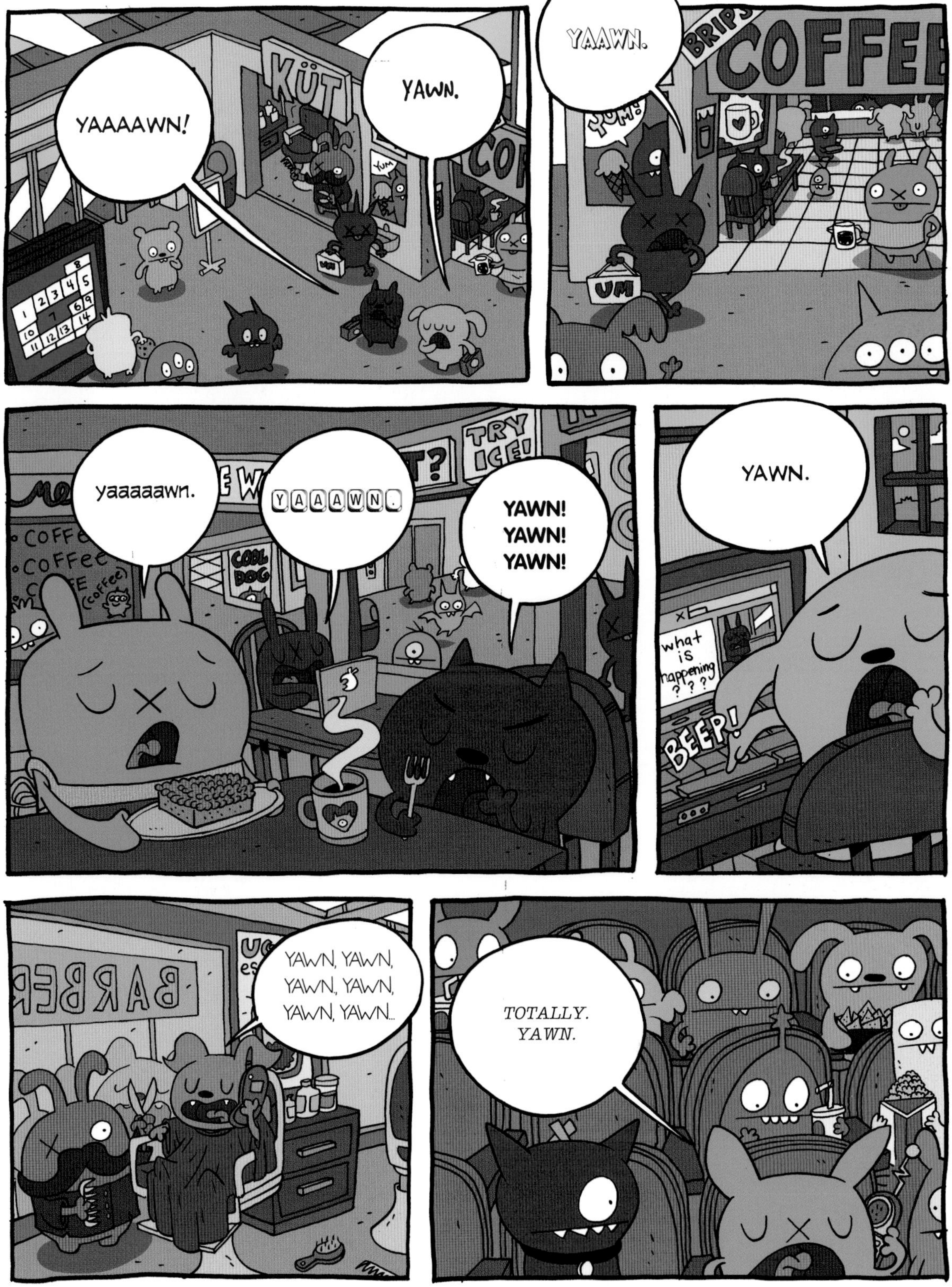
KÜT
YAAAAWN!
YAWN.
BRIPS
COFFEE
YAAWN.
UM
yaaaaawn.
YAAAWN.
TRY ICE!
COOL DOG
YAWN! YAWN! YAWN!
YAWN.
what is happening ???
BEEP!
YAWN, YAWN, YAWN, YAWN, YAWN, YAWN...
TOTALLY. YAWN.

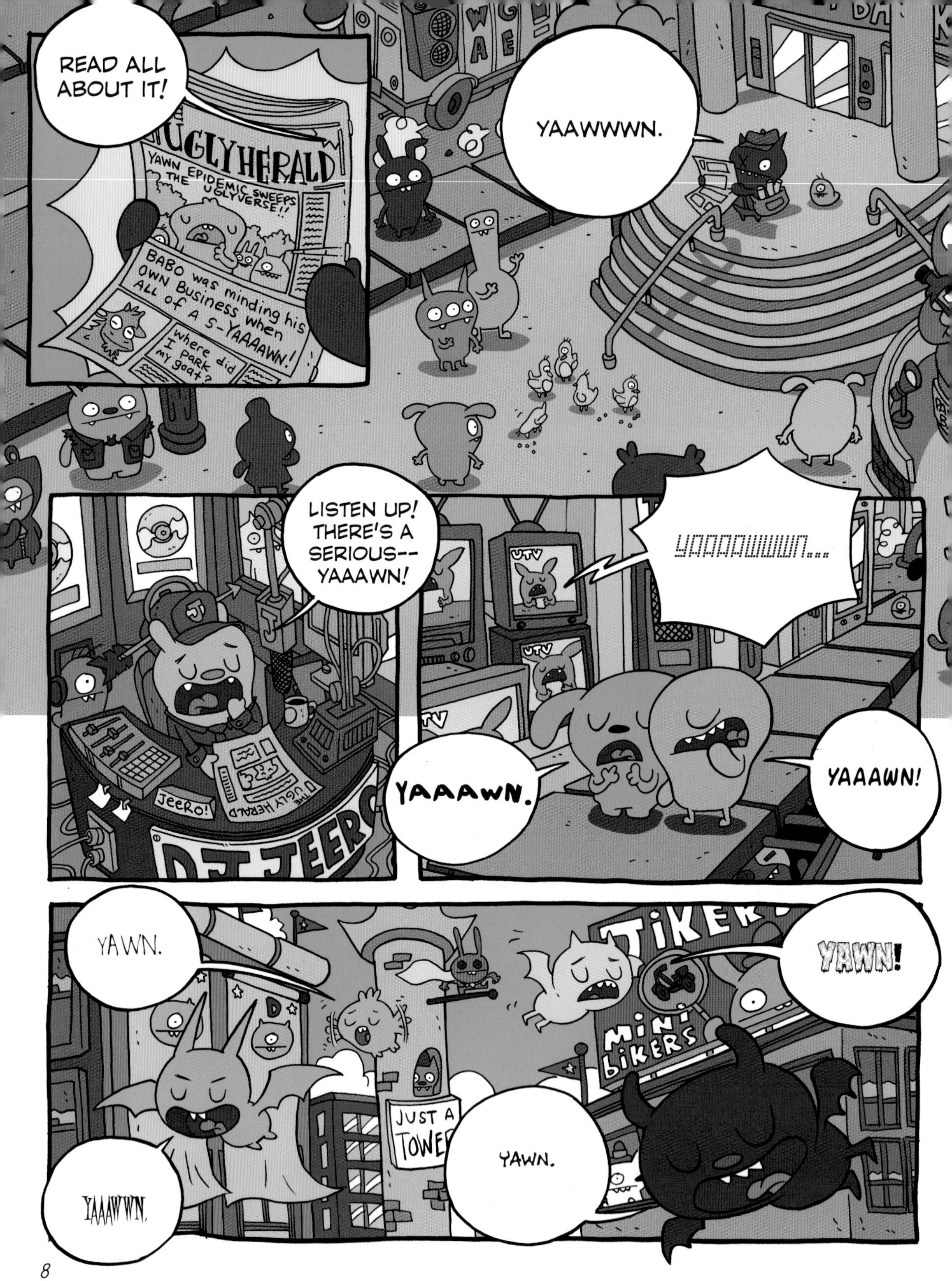
READ ALL ABOUT IT!
UGLYHERALD
YAWN EPIDEMIC SWEEPS THE UGLYVERSE!!
BABO was minding his OWN Business when ALL of A S-YAAAAWN!
where did I park my goat?
YAAWWWN.
LISTEN UP! THERE'S A SERIOUS-- YAAAWN!
JEERO!
THE UGLY HERALD
DJ JEERO
UTV
YAAAAWWWN...
YAAAWN.
YAAAWN!
YAWN.
TiKER
YAWN!
MiNi BiKERS
JUST A TOWER
YAWN.
YAAAWWN.

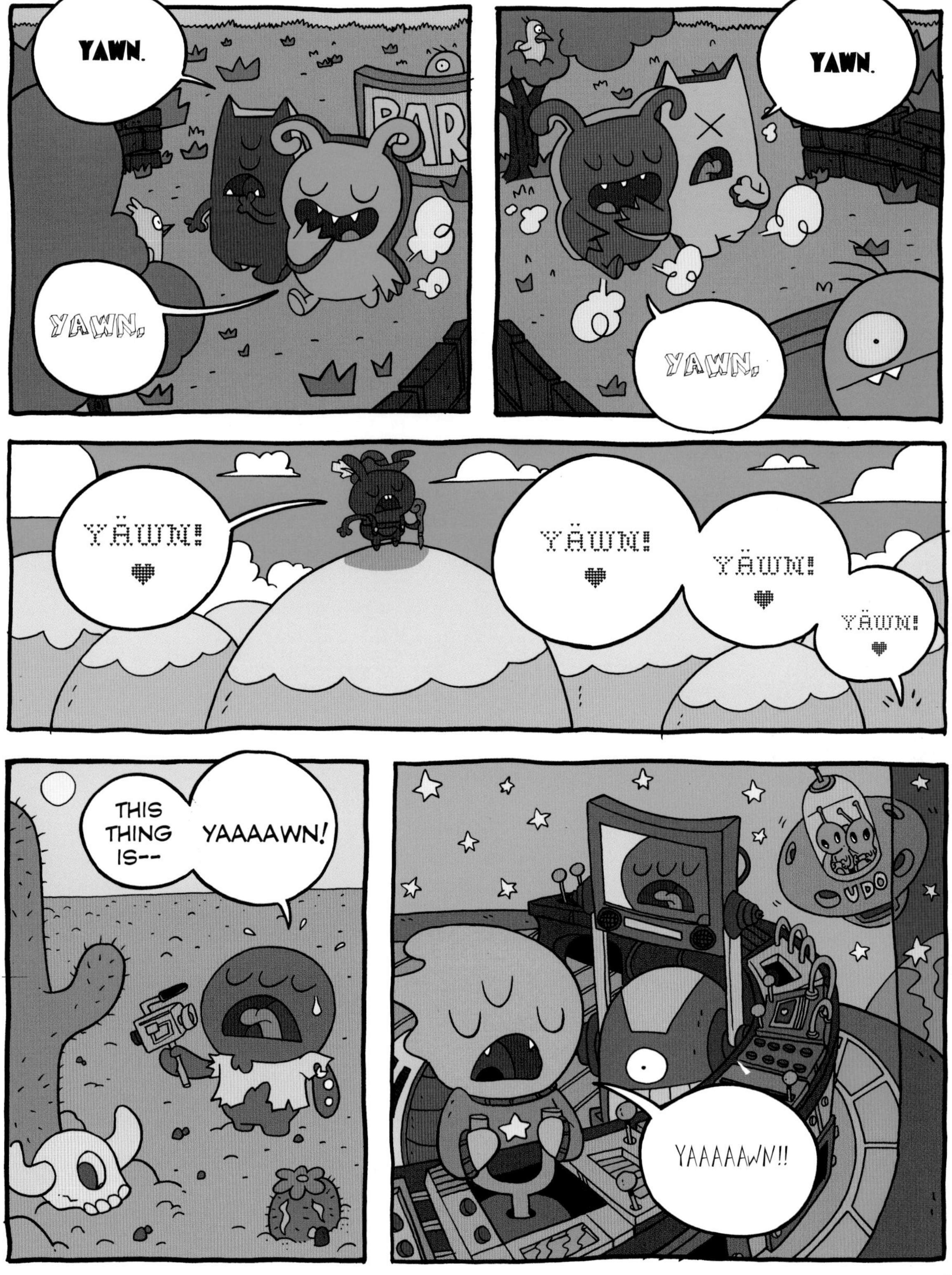
YAWN.
YAWN.
YAWN.
YAWN.
YÄWN!
YÄWN!
YÄWN!
YÄWN!
THIS THING IS--
YAAAAWN!
YAAAAAWN!!

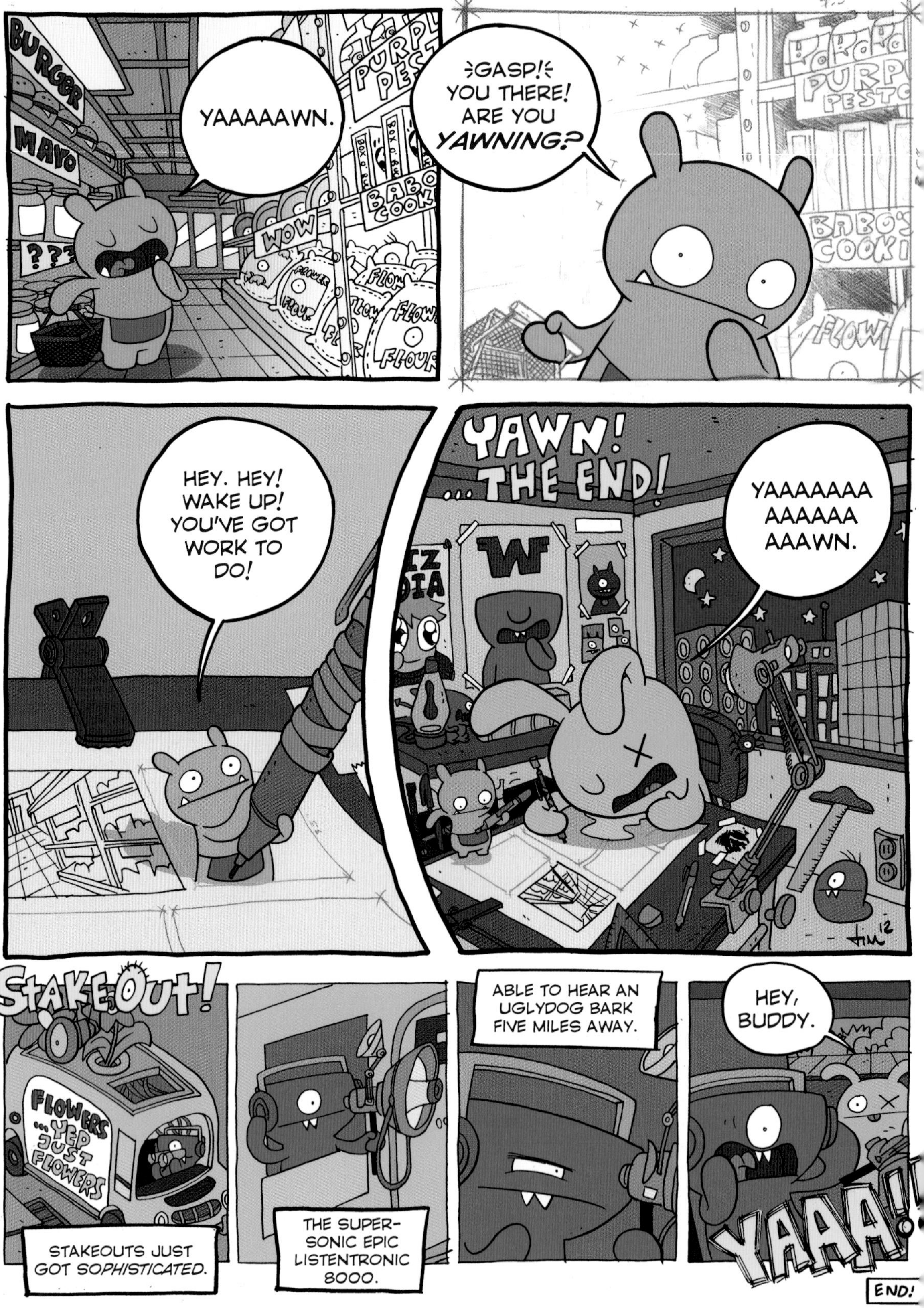
BURGER
MAYO
YAAAAAWN.
WOW
FLOUR
GASP!
YOU THERE!
ARE YOU
YAWNING?
HEY. HEY!
WAKE UP!
YOU'VE GOT
WORK TO
DO!
YAWN!
...THE END!
YAAAAAAA
AAAAAA
AAAWN.
STAKEOUT!
FLOWERS
...YEP
JUST
FLOWERS
STAKEOUTS JUST
GOT SOPHISTICATED.
THE SUPER-
SONIC EPIC
LISTENTRONIC
8000.
ABLE TO HEAR AN
UGLYDOG BARK
FIVE MILES AWAY.
HEY,
BUDDY.
YAAA!!
END!

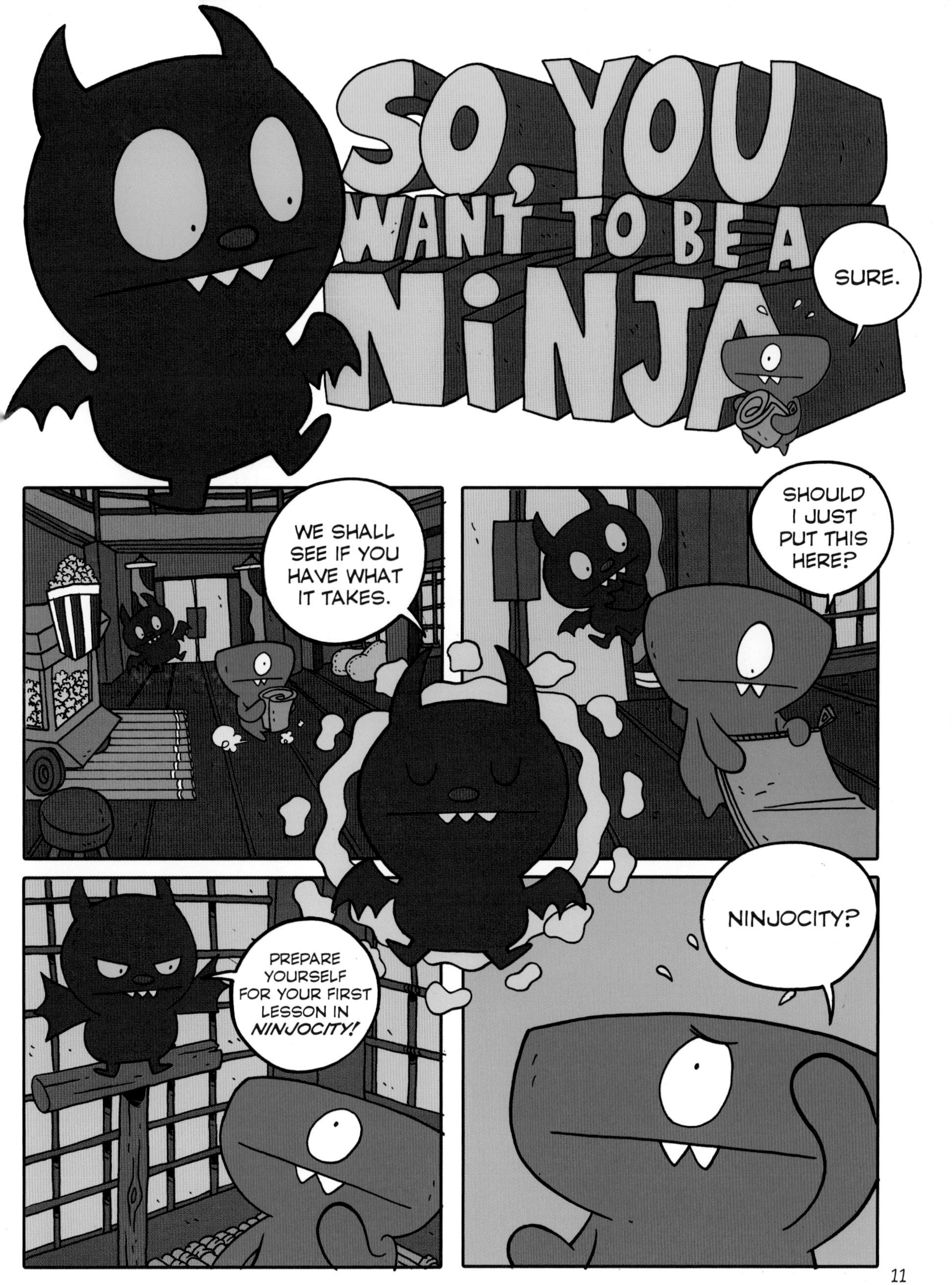
SO, YOU WANT TO BE A NINJA
SURE.
WE SHALL SEE IF YOU HAVE WHAT IT TAKES.
SHOULD I JUST PUT THIS HERE?
PREPARE YOURSELF FOR YOUR FIRST LESSON IN *NINJOCITY!*
NINJOCITY?

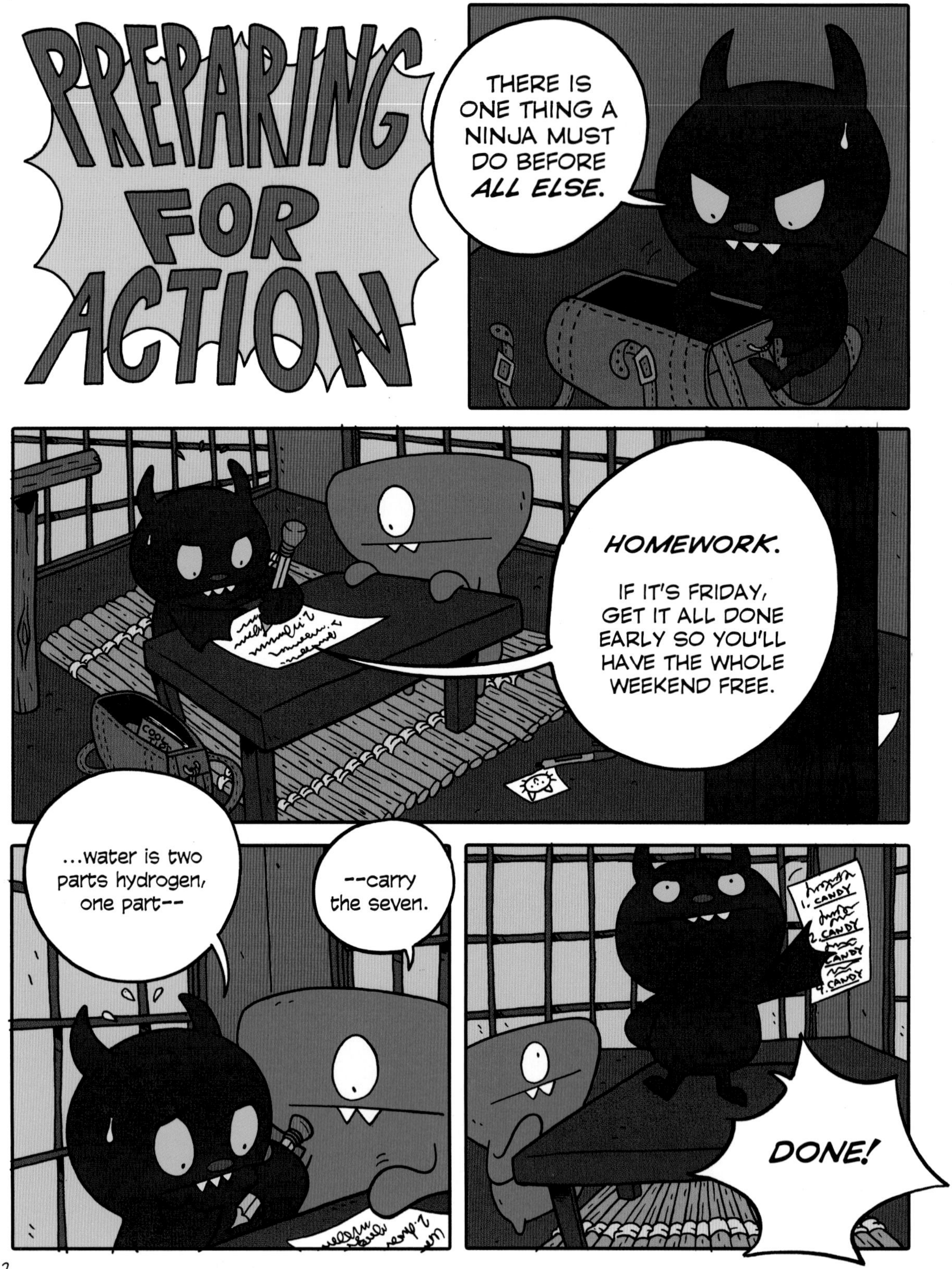
PREPARING FOR ACTION
THERE IS ONE THING A NINJA MUST DO BEFORE ALL ELSE.
HOMEWORK.
IF IT'S FRIDAY, GET IT ALL DONE EARLY SO YOU'LL HAVE THE WHOLE WEEKEND FREE.
...water is two parts hydrogen, one part--
--carry the seven.
DONE!

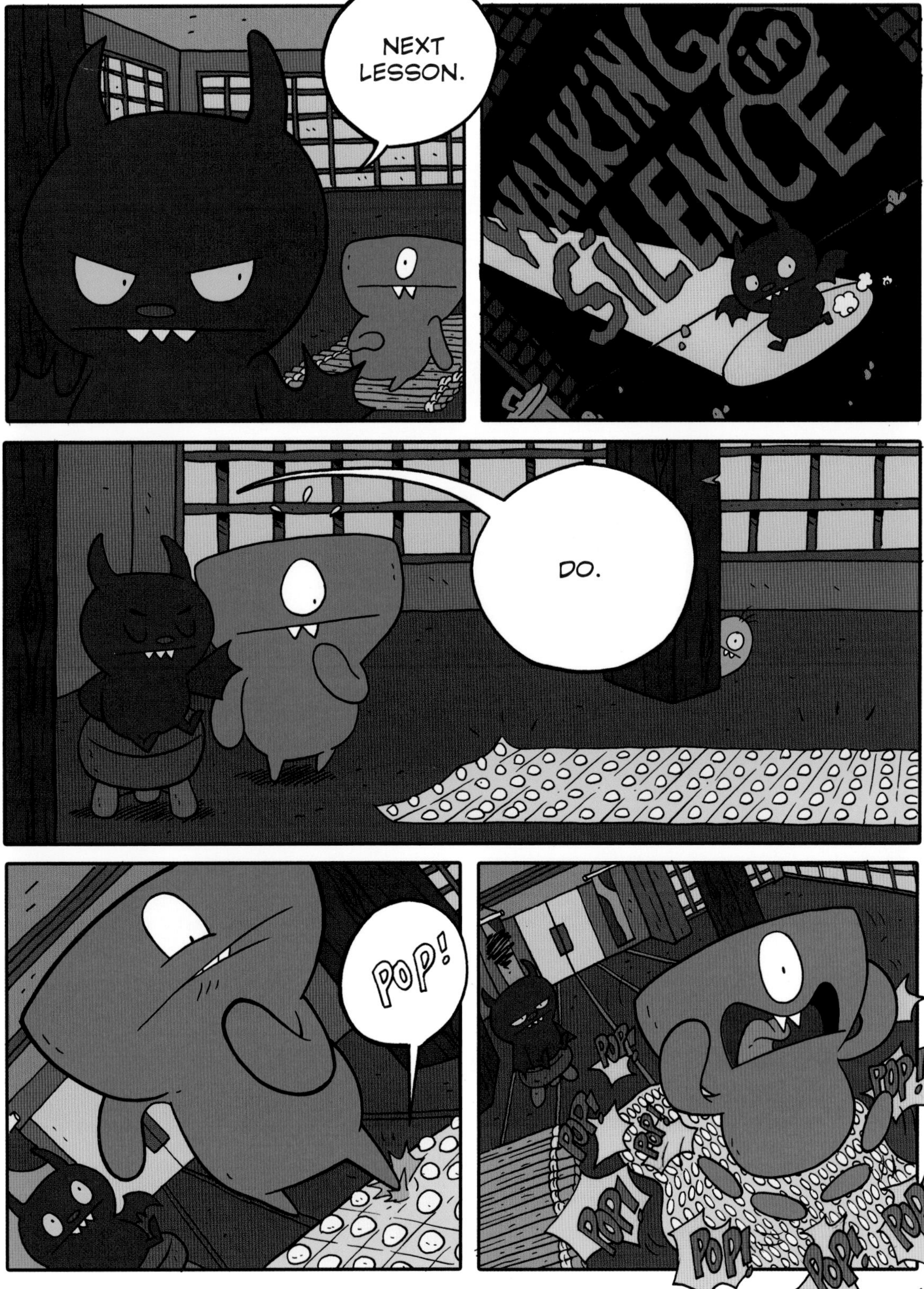
NEXT LESSON.
WALKING IN SILENCE
DO.
POP!
POP! POP! POP! POP! POP! POP! POP! POP!

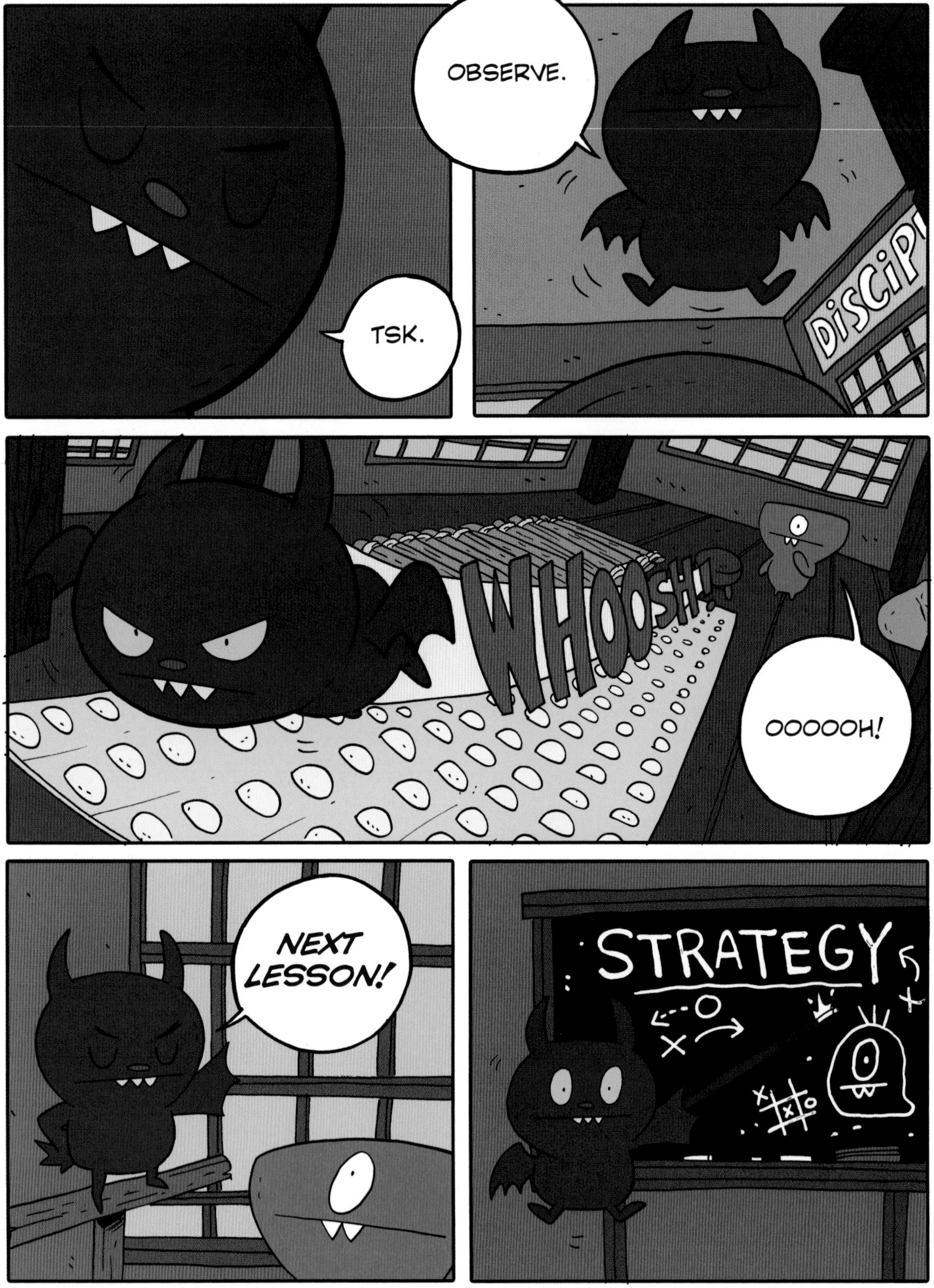
TSK.
OBSERVE.
DISCIP
WHOOSH!
OOOOOH!
NEXT LESSON!
STRATEGY

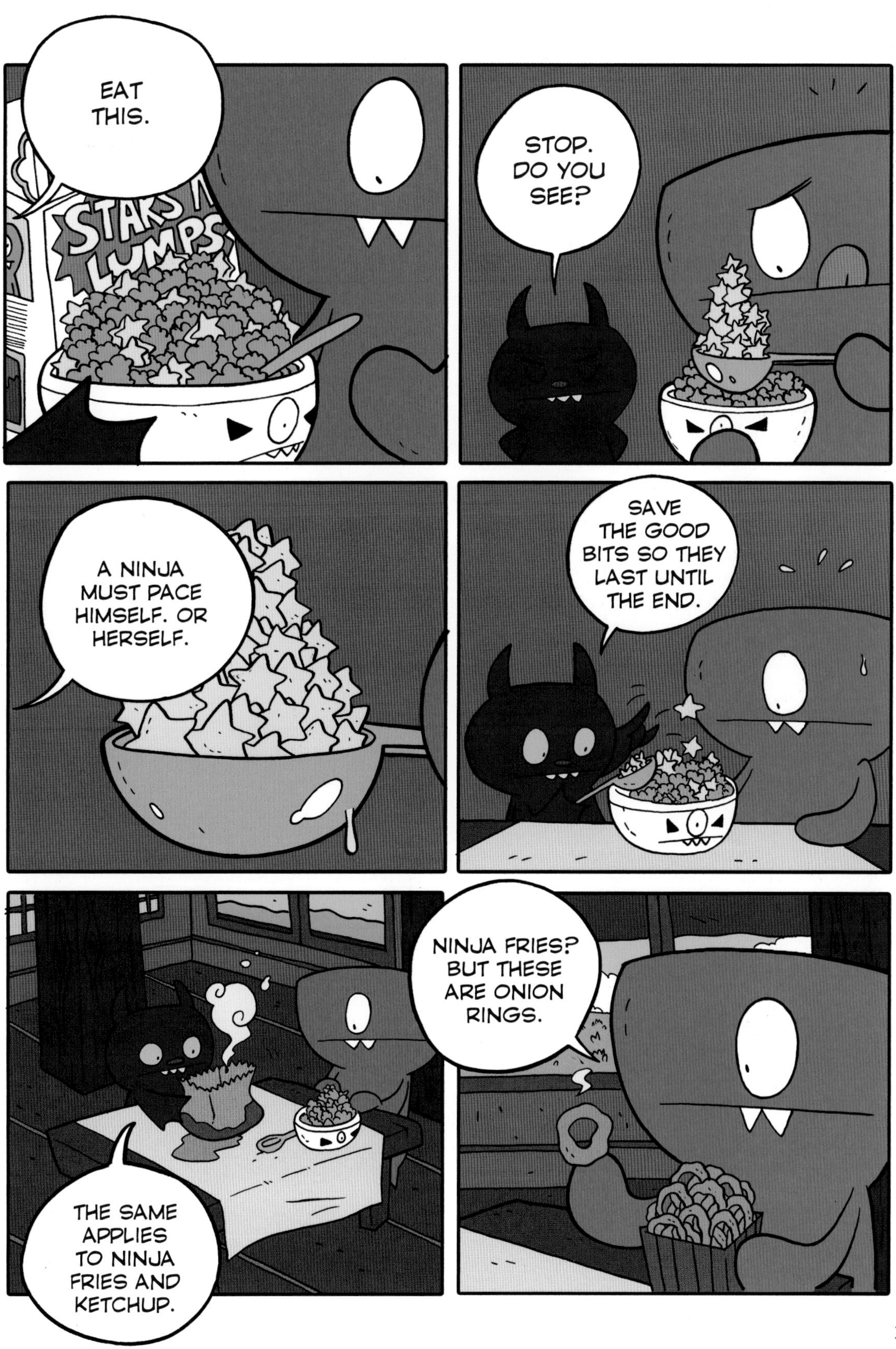
EAT THIS.
STARS N LUMPS
STOP. DO YOU SEE?
A NINJA MUST PACE HIMSELF. OR HERSELF.
SAVE THE GOOD BITS SO THEY LAST UNTIL THE END.
THE SAME APPLIES TO NINJA FRIES AND KETCHUP.
NINJA FRIES? BUT THESE ARE ONION RINGS.

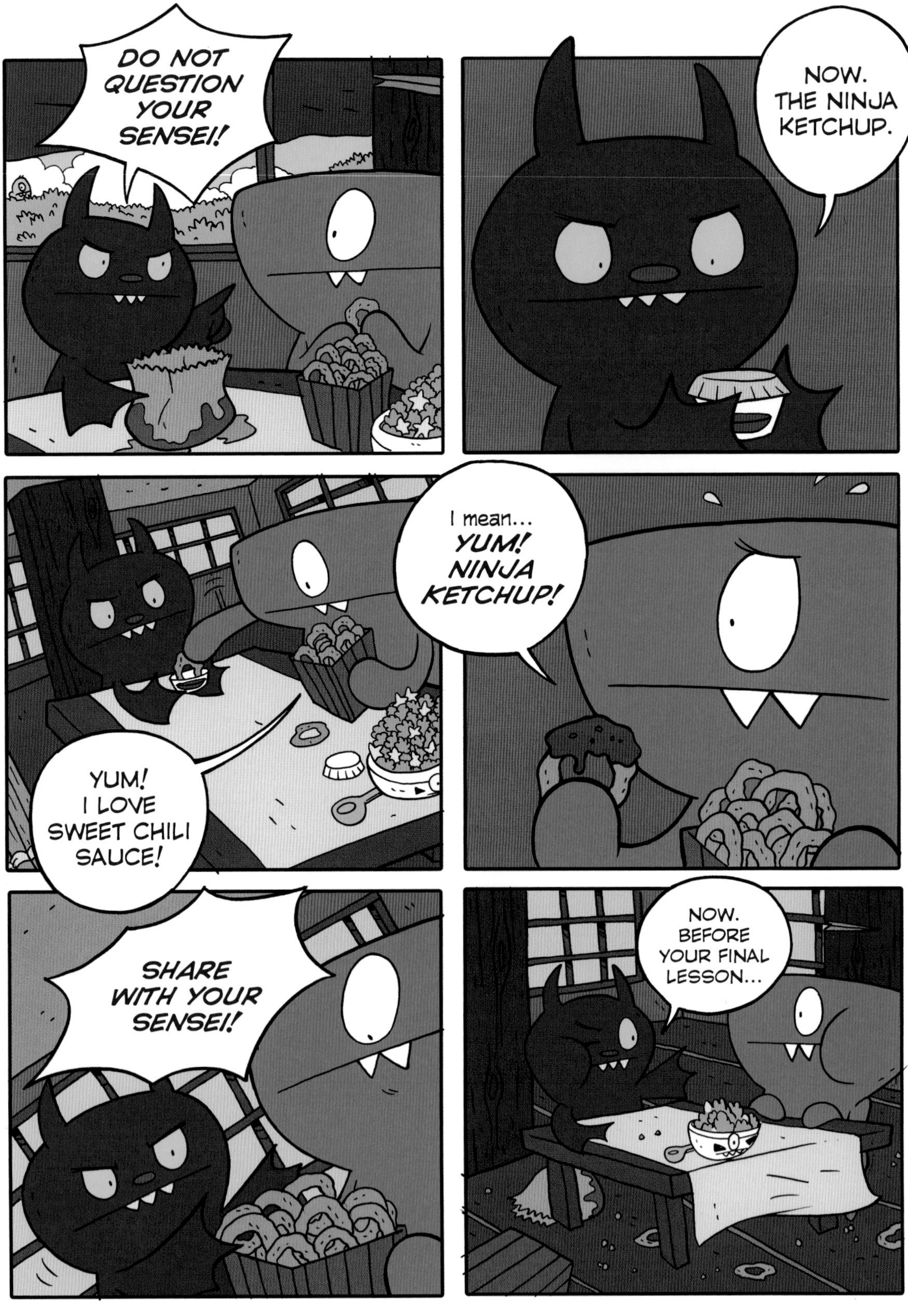
DO NOT QUESTION YOUR SENSEI!
NOW. THE NINJA KETCHUP.
I mean... YUM! NINJA KETCHUP!
YUM! I LOVE SWEET CHILI SAUCE!
SHARE WITH YOUR SENSEI!
NOW. BEFORE YOUR FINAL LESSON...

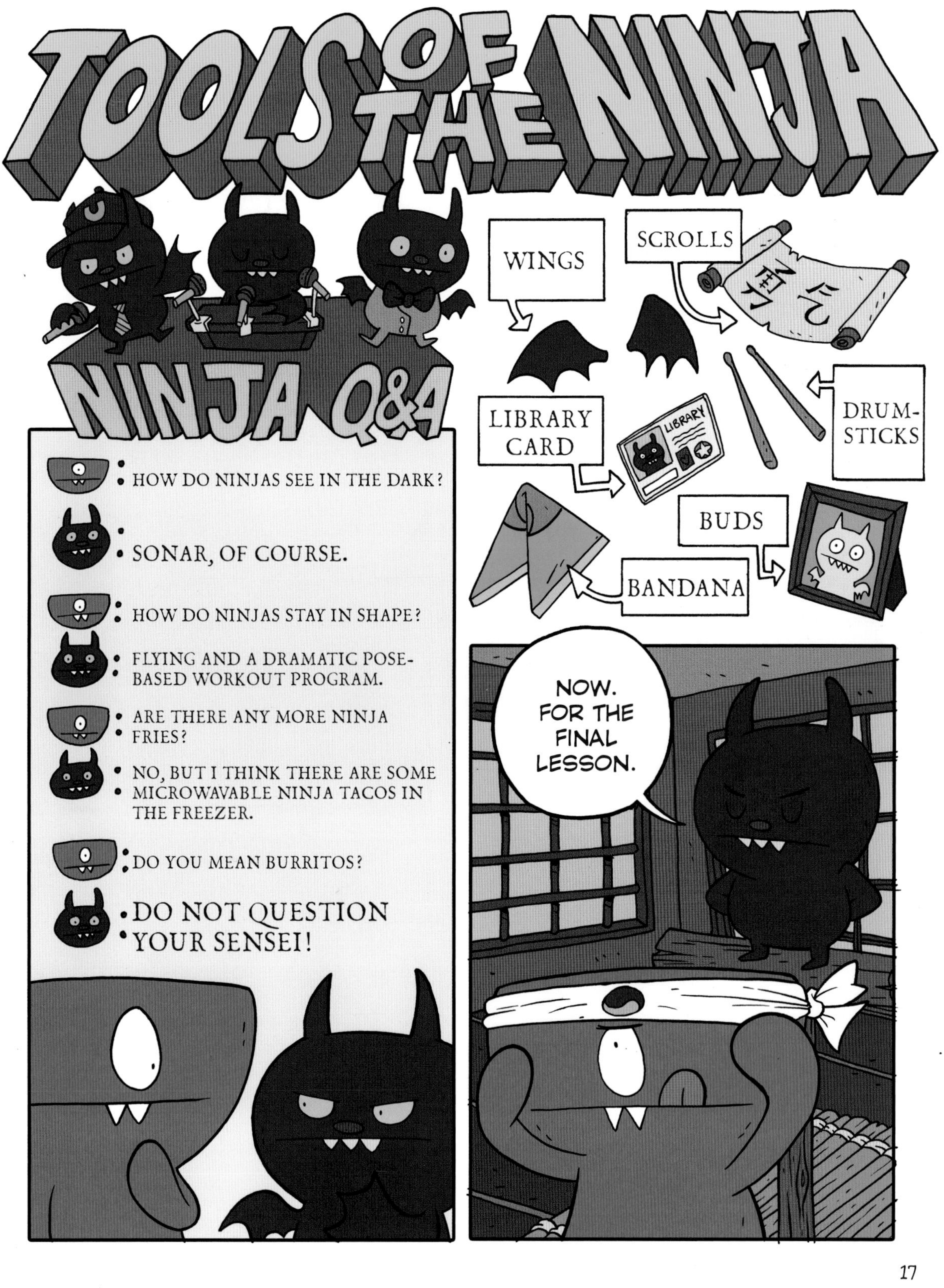
TOOLS OF THE NINJA
NINJA Q&A
HOW DO NINJAS SEE IN THE DARK?
SONAR, OF COURSE.
HOW DO NINJAS STAY IN SHAPE?
FLYING AND A DRAMATIC POSE-BASED WORKOUT PROGRAM.
ARE THERE ANY MORE NINJA FRIES?
NO, BUT I THINK THERE ARE SOME MICROWAVABLE NINJA TACOS IN THE FREEZER.
DO YOU MEAN BURRITOS?
DO NOT QUESTION YOUR SENSEI!
WINGS
SCROLLS
DRUM-STICKS
LIBRARY CARD
LIBRARY
BUDS
BANDANA
NOW. FOR THE FINAL LESSON.

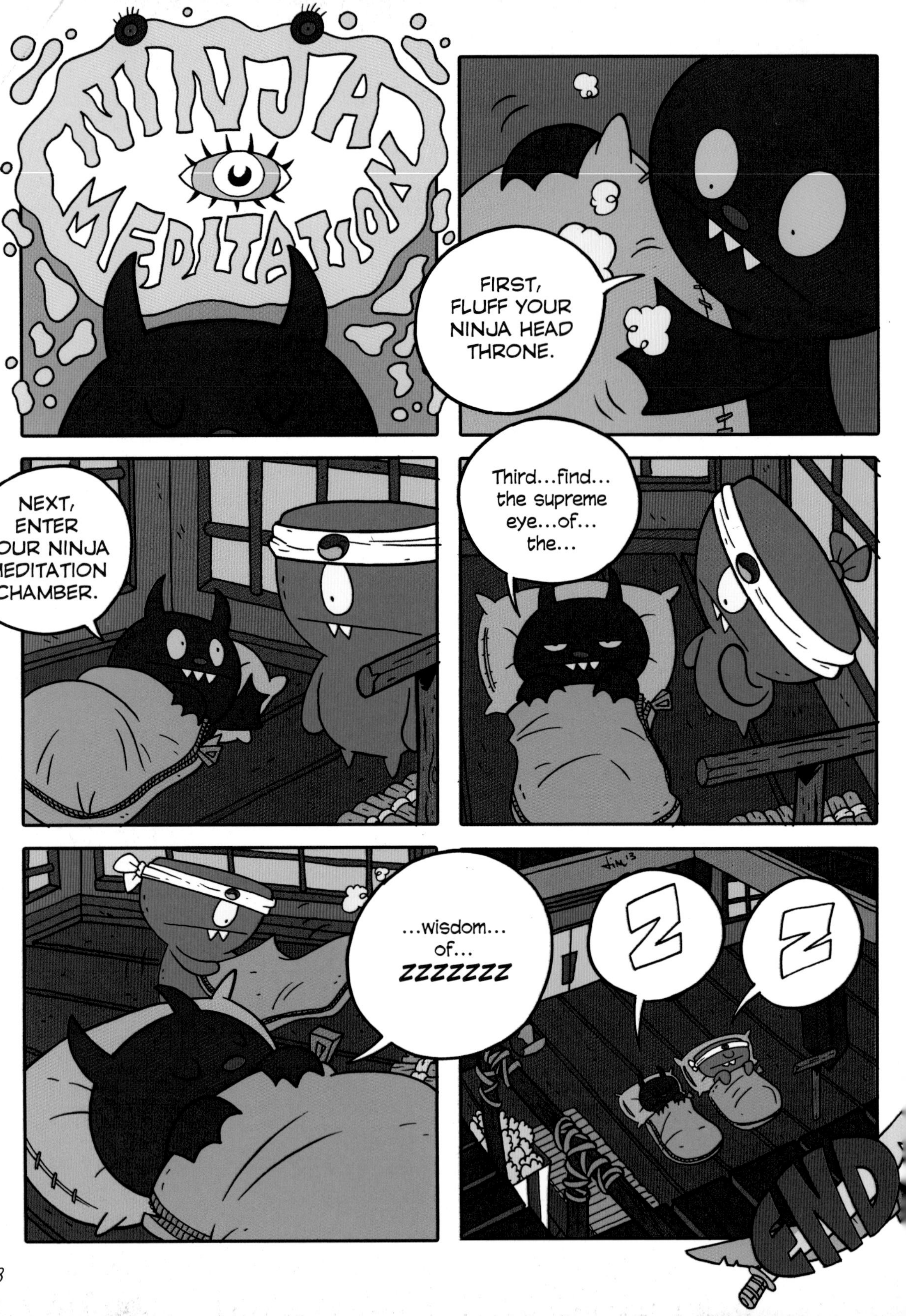
NINJA MEDITATION
FIRST, FLUFF YOUR NINJA HEAD THRONE.
NEXT, ENTER YOUR NINJA MEDITATION CHAMBER.
Third...find... the supreme eye...of... the...
...wisdom... of... ZZZZZZZ
Z
Z
END

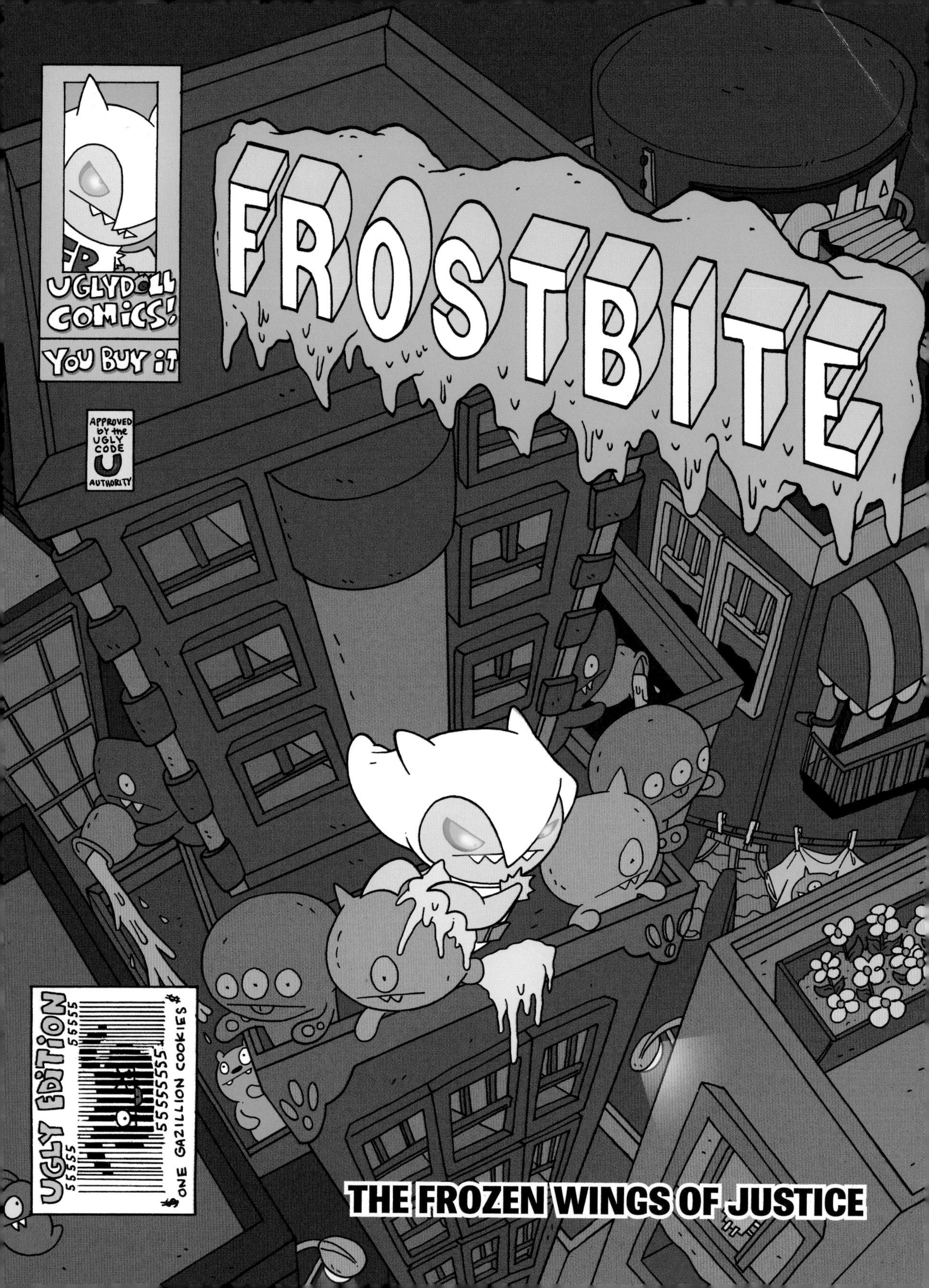
UGLYDOLL COMICS!
YOU BUY IT
FROSTBITE
APPROVED by the UGLY CODE U AUTHORITY
UGLY EDITION
ONE GAZILLION COOKIES
THE FROZEN WINGS OF JUSTICE

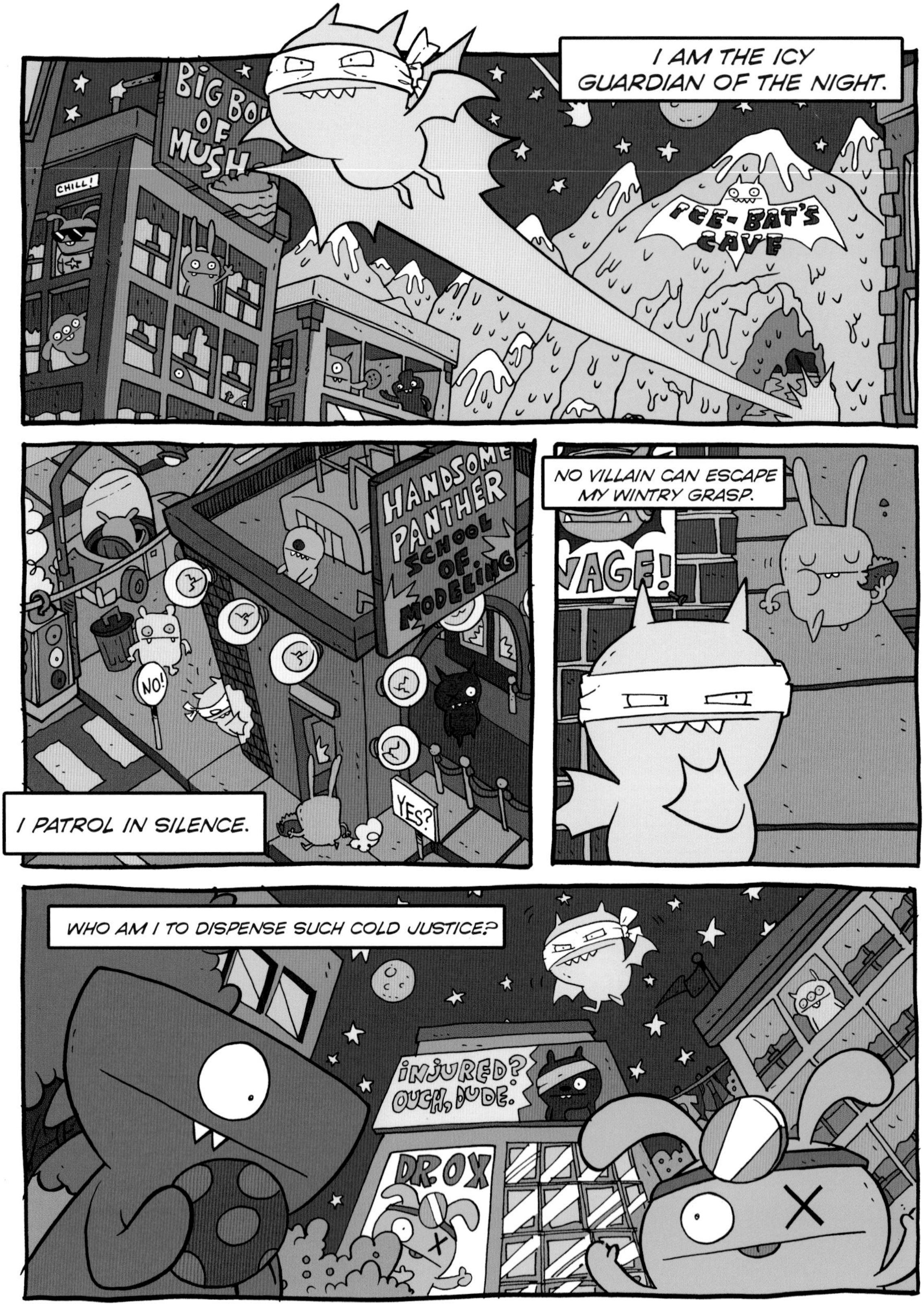
I AM THE ICY GUARDIAN OF THE NIGHT.
BIG BOWL OF MUSH
CHILL!
ICE-BAT'S CAVE
HANDSOME PANTHER SCHOOL OF MODELING
NO!
YES?
I PATROL IN SILENCE.
NO VILLAIN CAN ESCAPE MY WINTRY GRASP.
WHO AM I TO DISPENSE SUCH COLD JUSTICE?
INJURED? OUCH, DUDE.
DR. OX

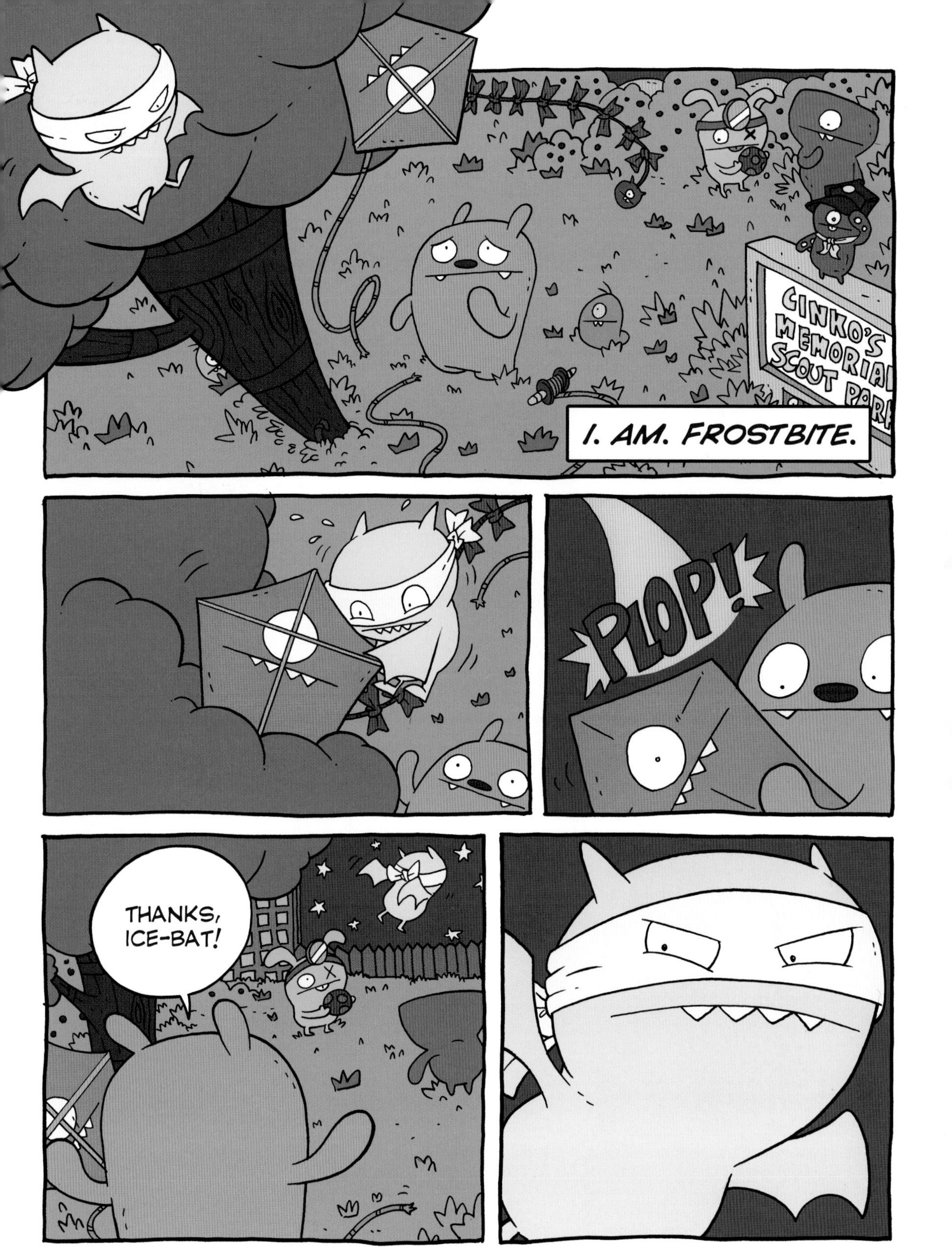
CINKO'S MEMORIAL SCOUT PARK
I. AM. FROSTBITE.
PLOP!
THANKS, ICE-BAT!

TO BE CONTINUED...

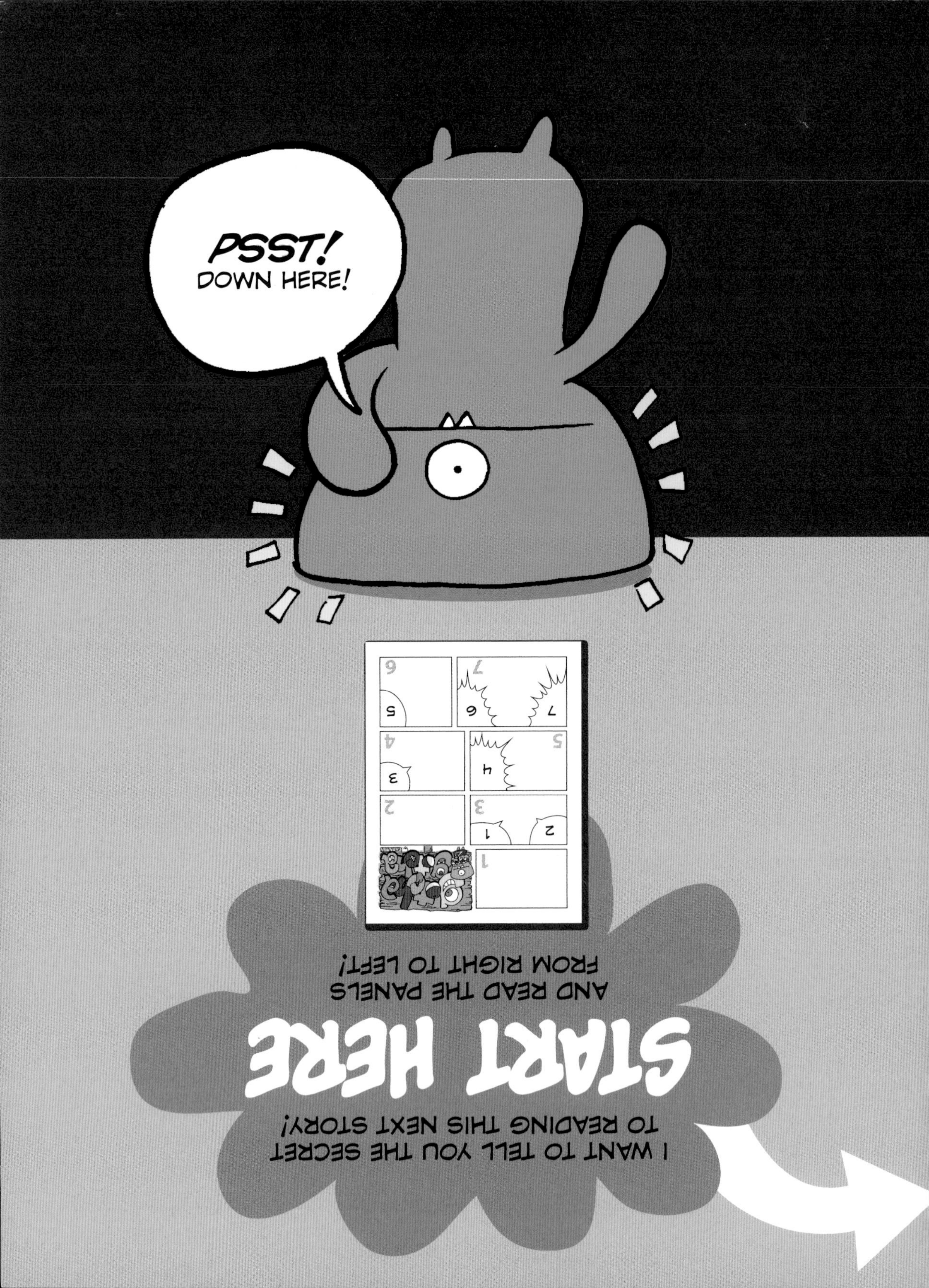
PSST! DOWN HERE!
I WANT TO TELL YOU THE SECRET TO READING THIS NEXT STORY!
START HERE
AND READ THE PANELS FROM RIGHT TO LEFT!

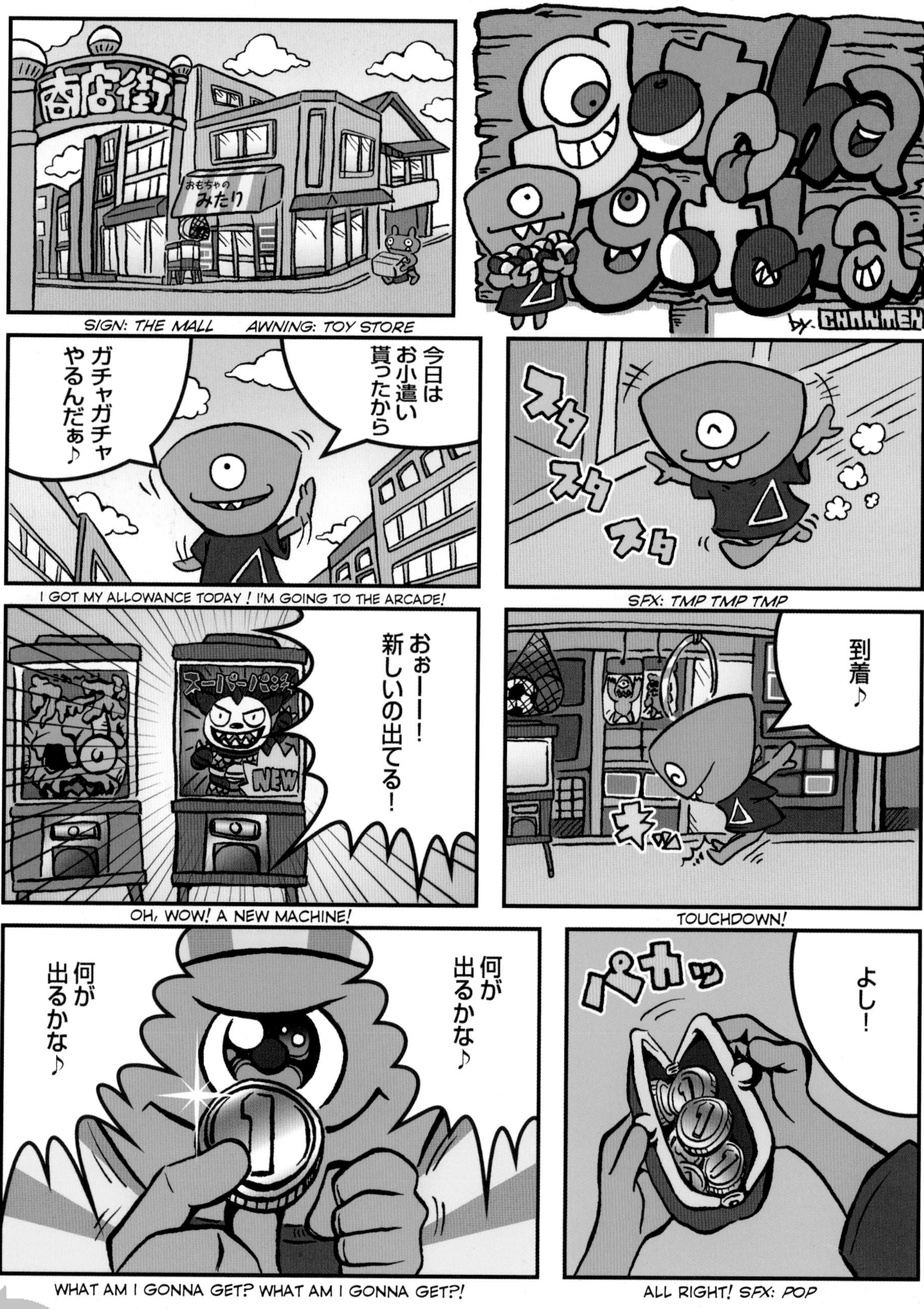
商店街
おもちゃの
みたり
gacha gacha
by CHANMEH
SIGN: THE MALL AWNING: TOY STORE
今日はお小遣い貰ったから
ガチャガチャやるんだぁ♪
I GOT MY ALLOWANCE TODAY ! I'M GOING TO THE ARCADE!
スタ スタ スタ
SFX: TMP TMP TMP
おぉーーー!新しいの出てる!
スーパーパンチ
NEW
OH, WOW! A NEW MACHINE!
到着♪
TOUCHDOWN!
何が出るかな♪
何が出るかな♪
WHAT AM I GONNA GET? WHAT AM I GONNA GET?!
パカッ
よし!
ALL RIGHT! SFX: POP

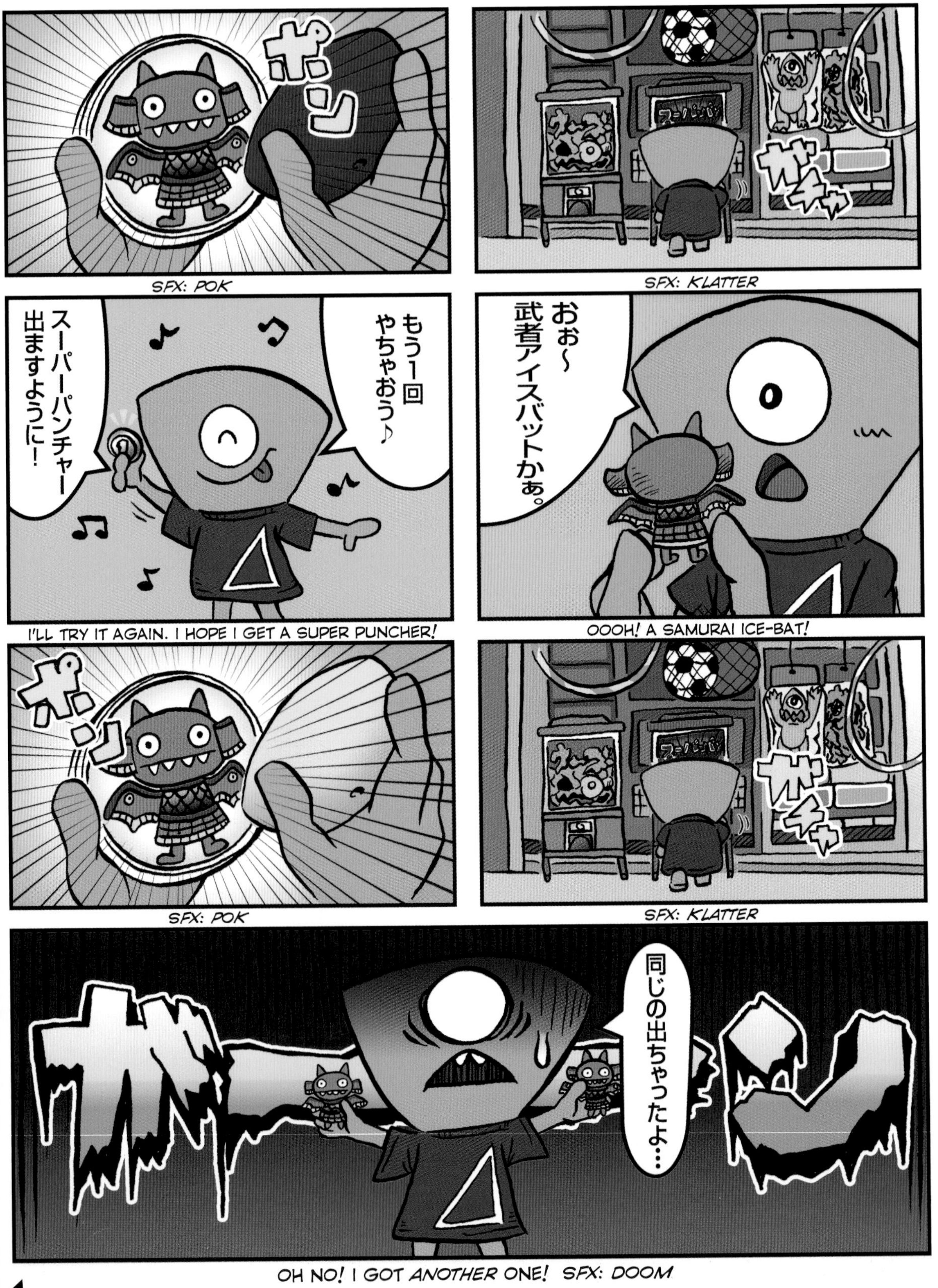
ガチャ
SFX: KLATTER
ポン
SFX: POK
おぉ~ 武者アイスバットかぁ。
OOOH! A SAMURAI ICE-BAT!
もう1回 やちゃおう♪
スーパーパンチャー 出ますように!
I'LL TRY IT AGAIN. I HOPE I GET A SUPER PUNCHER!
ガチャ
SFX: KLATTER
ポン
SFX: POK
同じの出ちゃったよ…
OH NO! I GOT ANOTHER ONE! SFX: DOOM

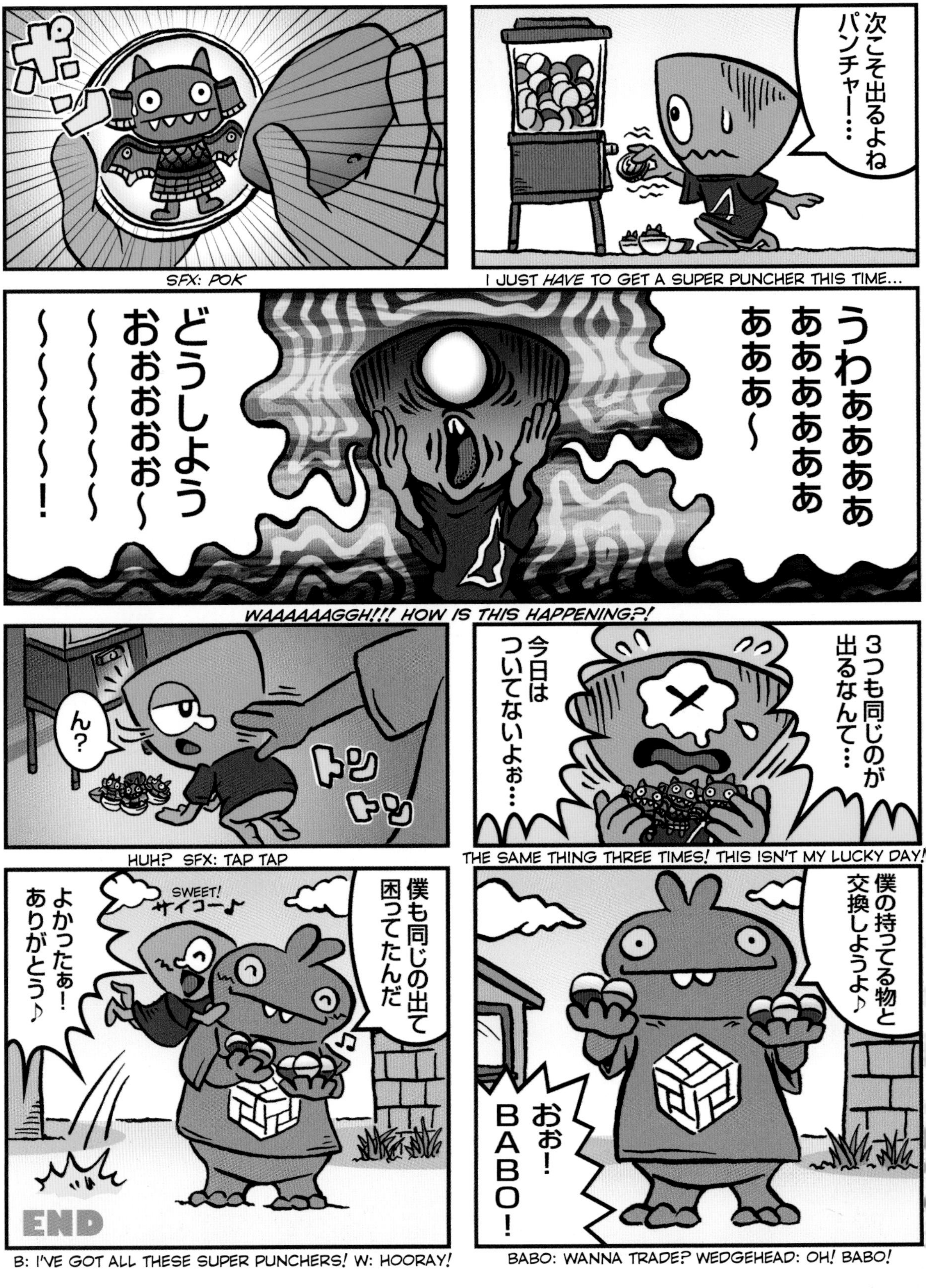

次こそ出るよね
パンチャー…
I JUST HAVE TO GET A SUPER PUNCHER THIS TIME...
ポンッ
SFX: POK
うわぁああああああああ～
どうしようおおおおお～～～～～～～～！
WAAAAAAAGGH!!! HOW IS THIS HAPPENING?!
3つも同じのが出るなんて…
今日はついてないよぉ…
THE SAME THING THREE TIMES! THIS ISN'T MY LUCKY DAY!
ん？
トン トン
HUH? SFX: TAP TAP
僕の持ってる物と交換しようよ♪
おぉ！BABO！
BABO: WANNA TRADE? WEDGEHEAD: OH! BABO!
僕も同じの出て困ってたんだ
SWEET!
サイコー♪
よかったぁ！ありがとう♪
END
B: I'VE GOT ALL THESE SUPER PUNCHERS! W: HOORAY!

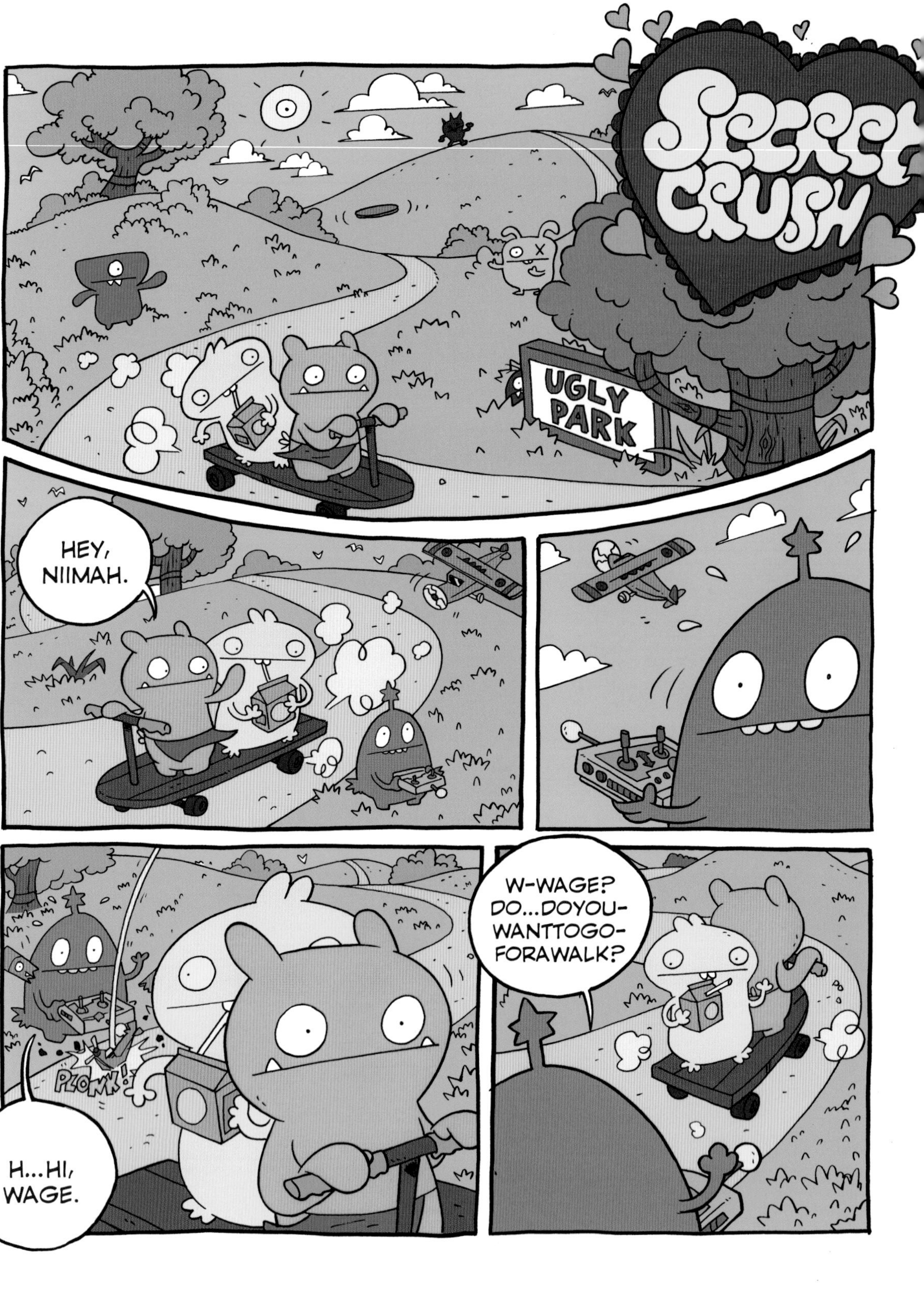
CRUSH
UGLY PARK
HEY, NIIMAH.
PLONK!
H...HI, WAGE.
W-WAGE? DO...DOYOU-WANTTOGO-FORAWALK?

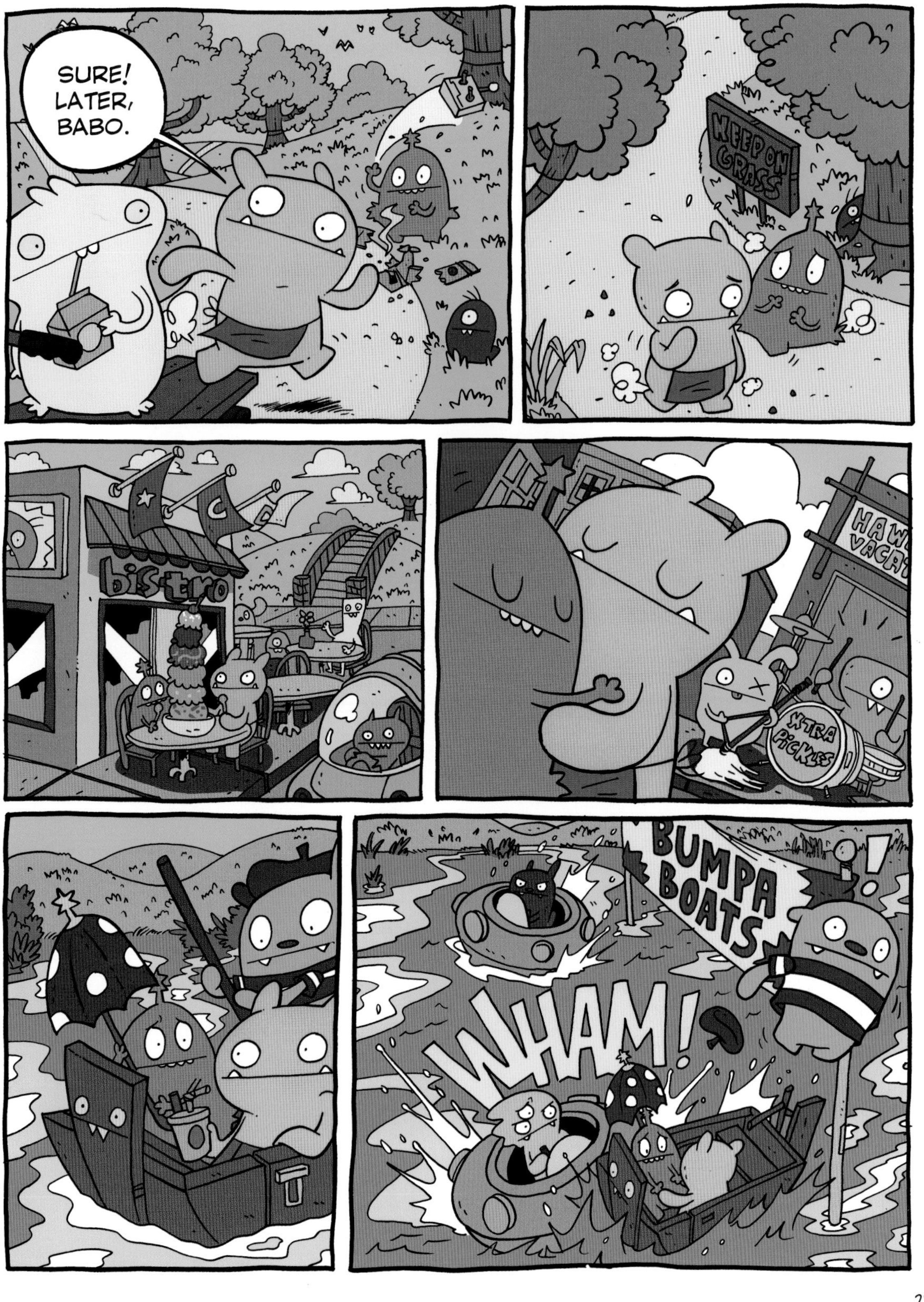
SURE! LATER, BABO.
KEEP ON GRASS
bistro
HAW VACA
XTRA PICKLES
BUMPA BOATS
WHAM!
!

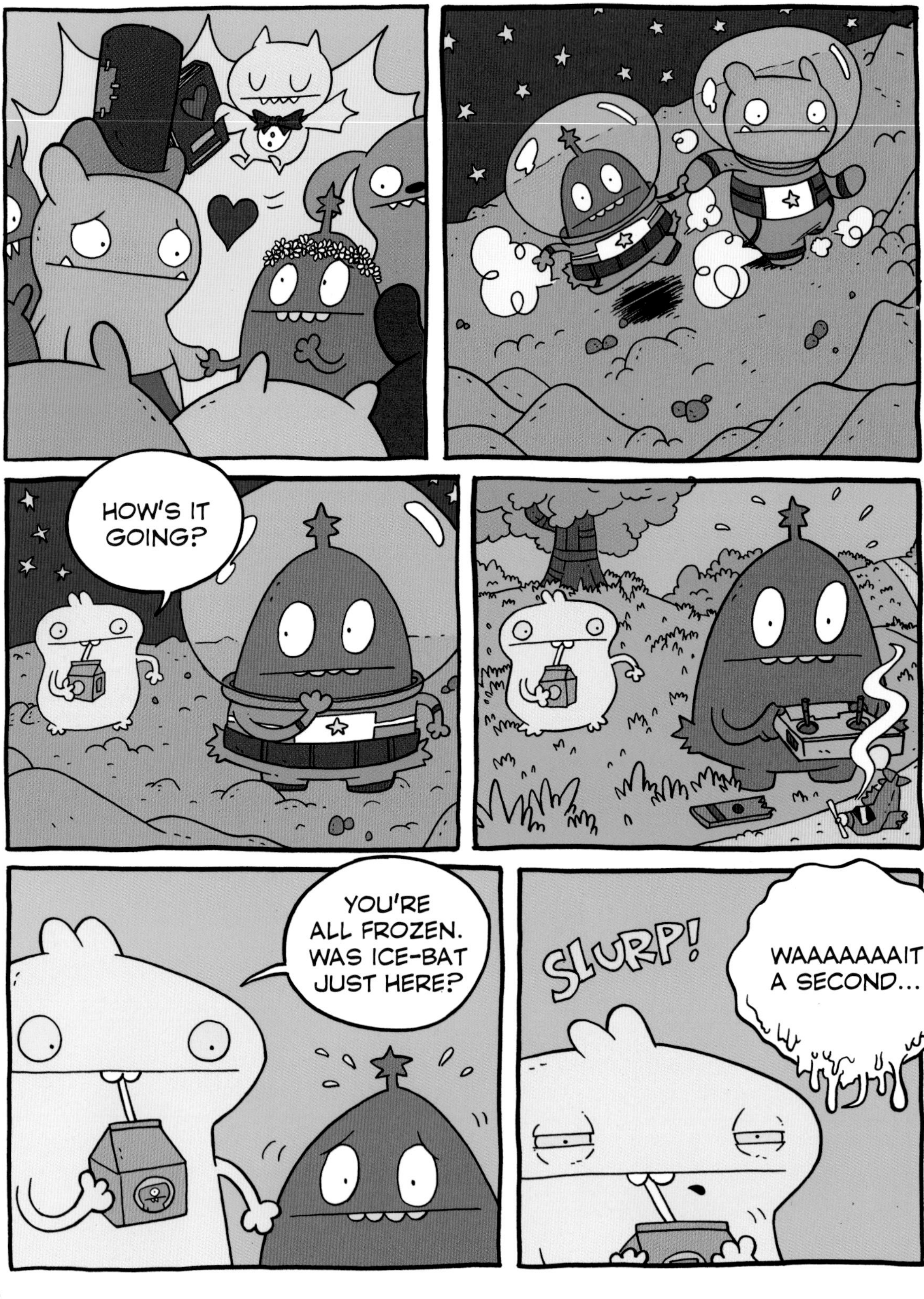
HOW'S IT GOING?
YOU'RE ALL FROZEN. WAS ICE-BAT JUST HERE?
SLURP!
WAAAAAAAIT A SECOND...

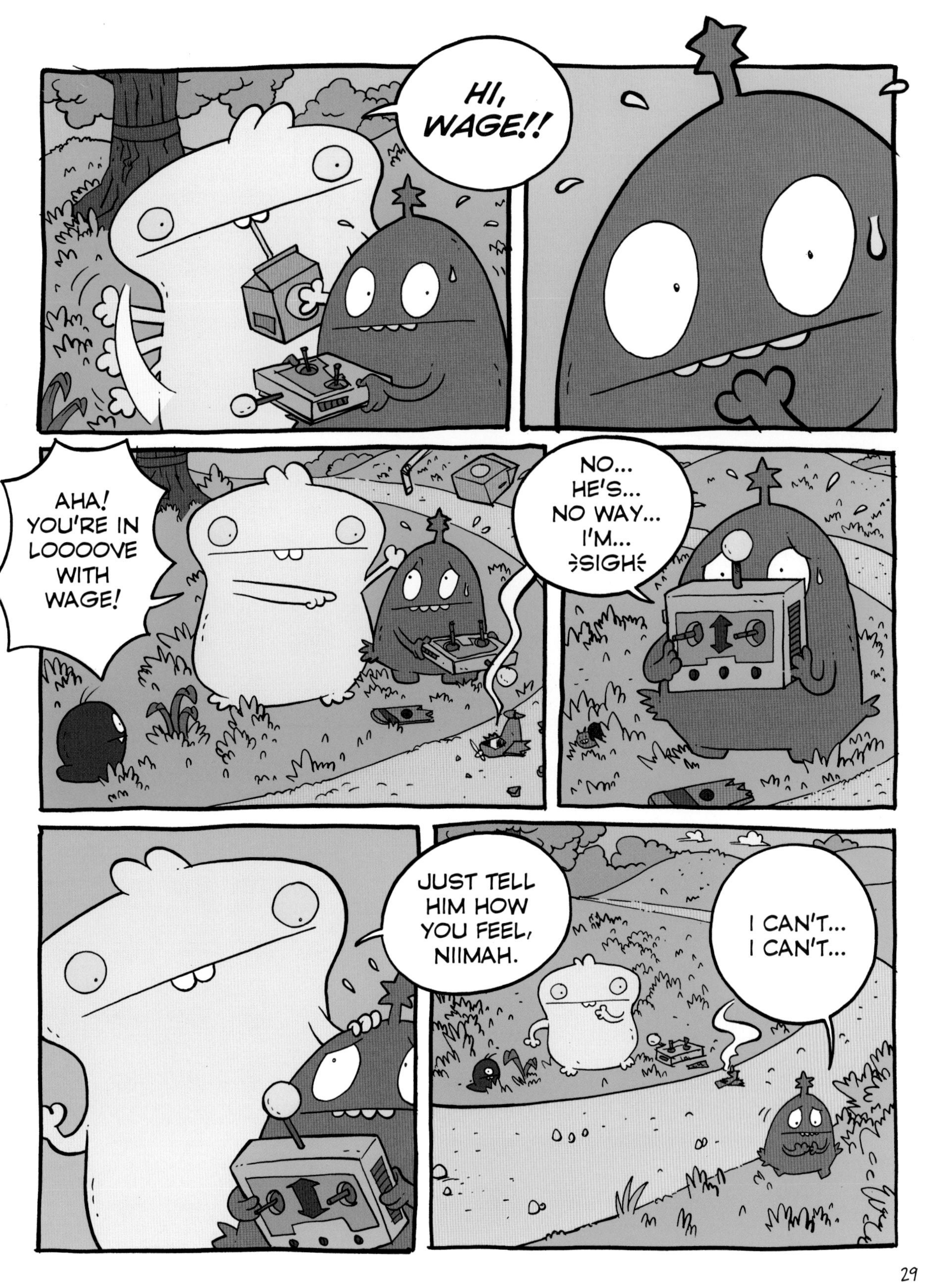
HI, WAGE!!
AHA! YOU'RE IN LOOOOVE WITH WAGE!
NO... HE'S... NO WAY... I'M... SIGH
JUST TELL HIM HOW YOU FEEL, NIIMAH.
I CAN'T... I CAN'T...

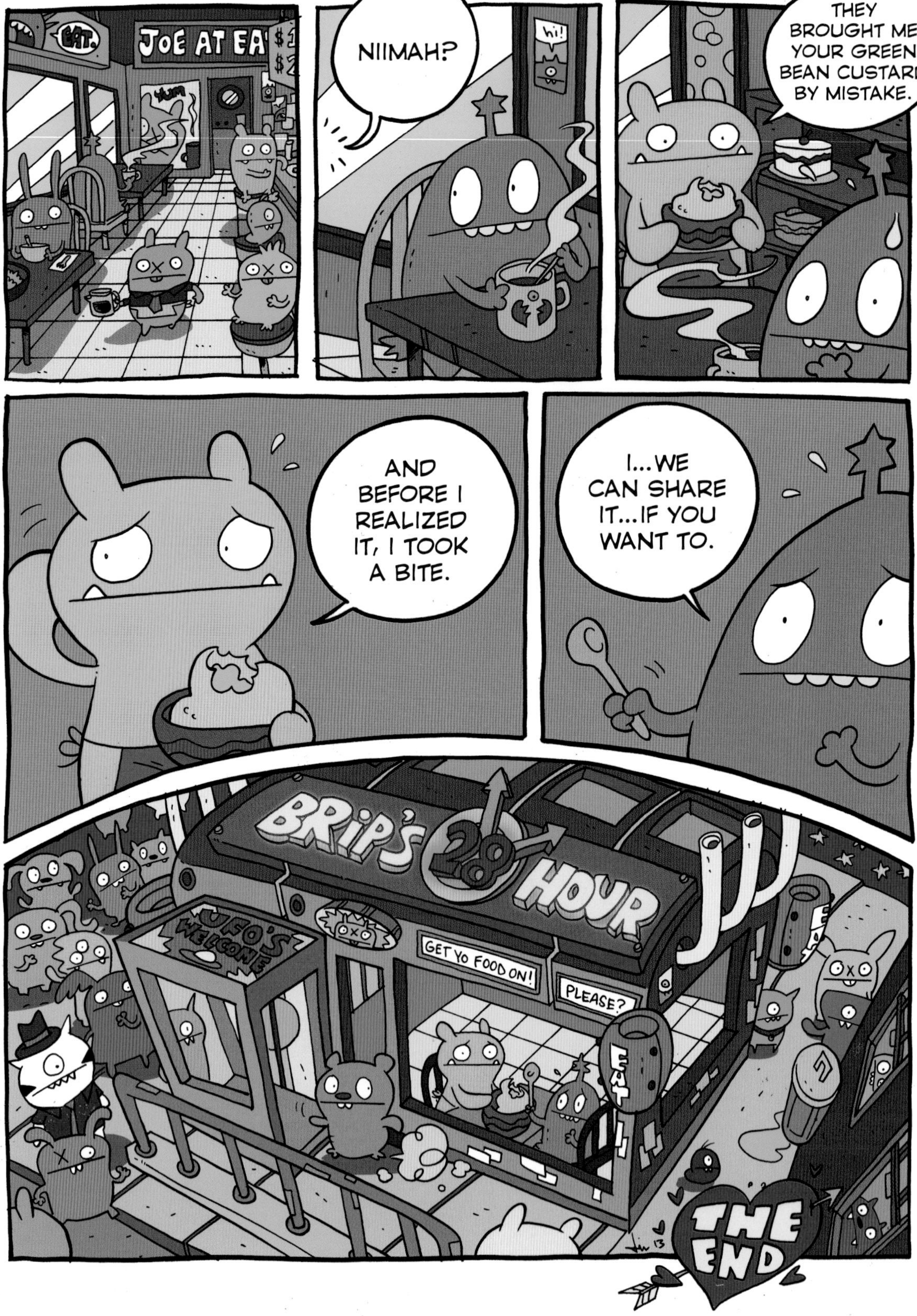

EAT.
JOE AT EA
YUM
NIIMAH?
hi!
THEY BROUGHT ME YOUR GREEN BEAN CUSTARD BY MISTAKE.
AND BEFORE I REALIZED IT, I TOOK A BITE.
I...WE CAN SHARE IT...IF YOU WANT TO.
BRiP'S 28 HOUR
UFO'S WELCOME
GET YO FOOD ON!
PLEASE?
EAT
THE END

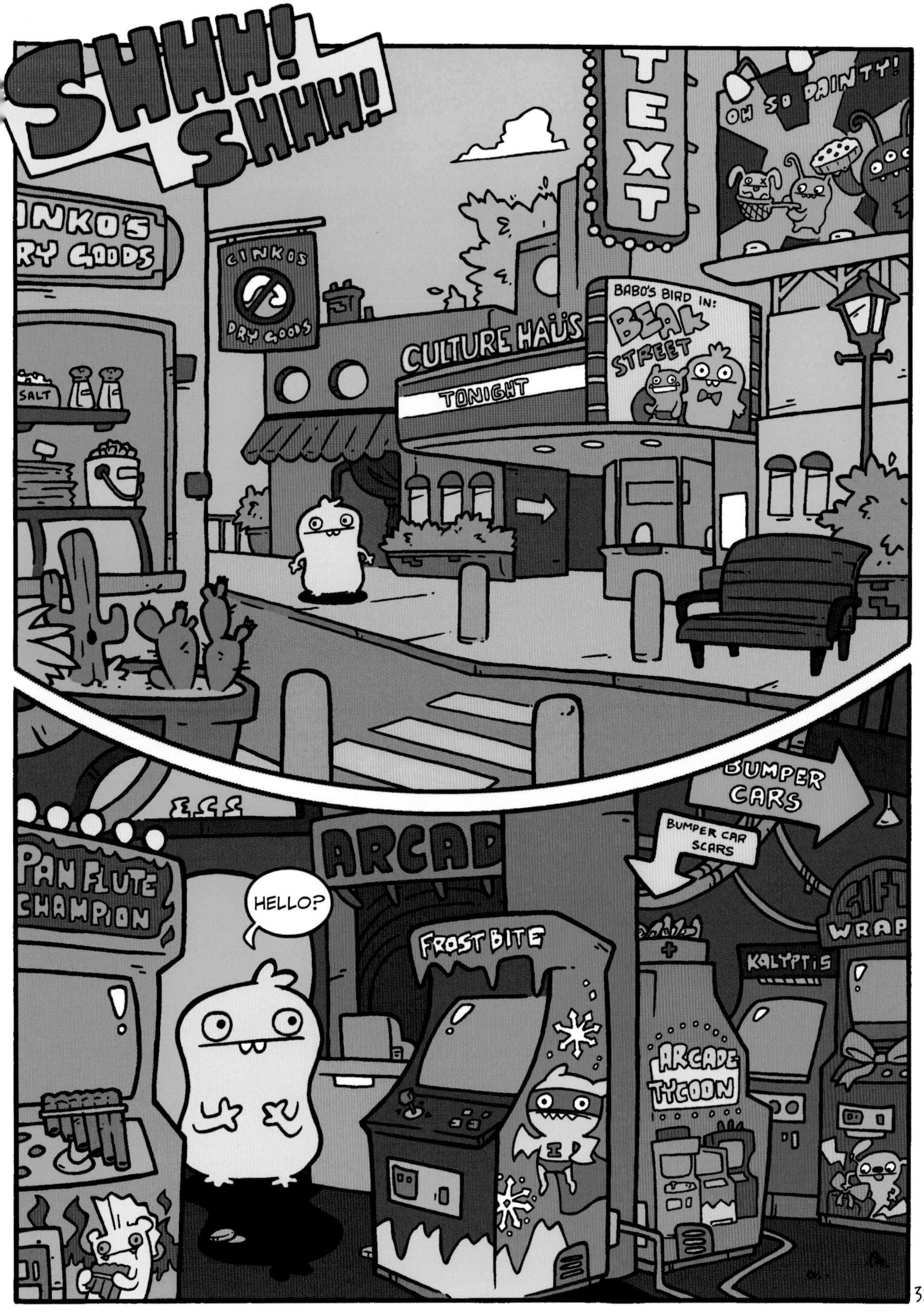
SHHH! SHHH!
...INKO'S ...RY GOODS
CINKOS DRY GOODS
SALT
TEXT
OH SO PAINTY!
CULTURE HAUS
TONIGHT
BABO'S BIRD IN: BEAK STREET
BUMPER CARS
BUMPER CAR SCARS
ARCAD...
PAN FLUTE CHAMPION
HELLO?
FROST BITE
KALYPTIS
ARCADE TYCOON
GIFT WRAP

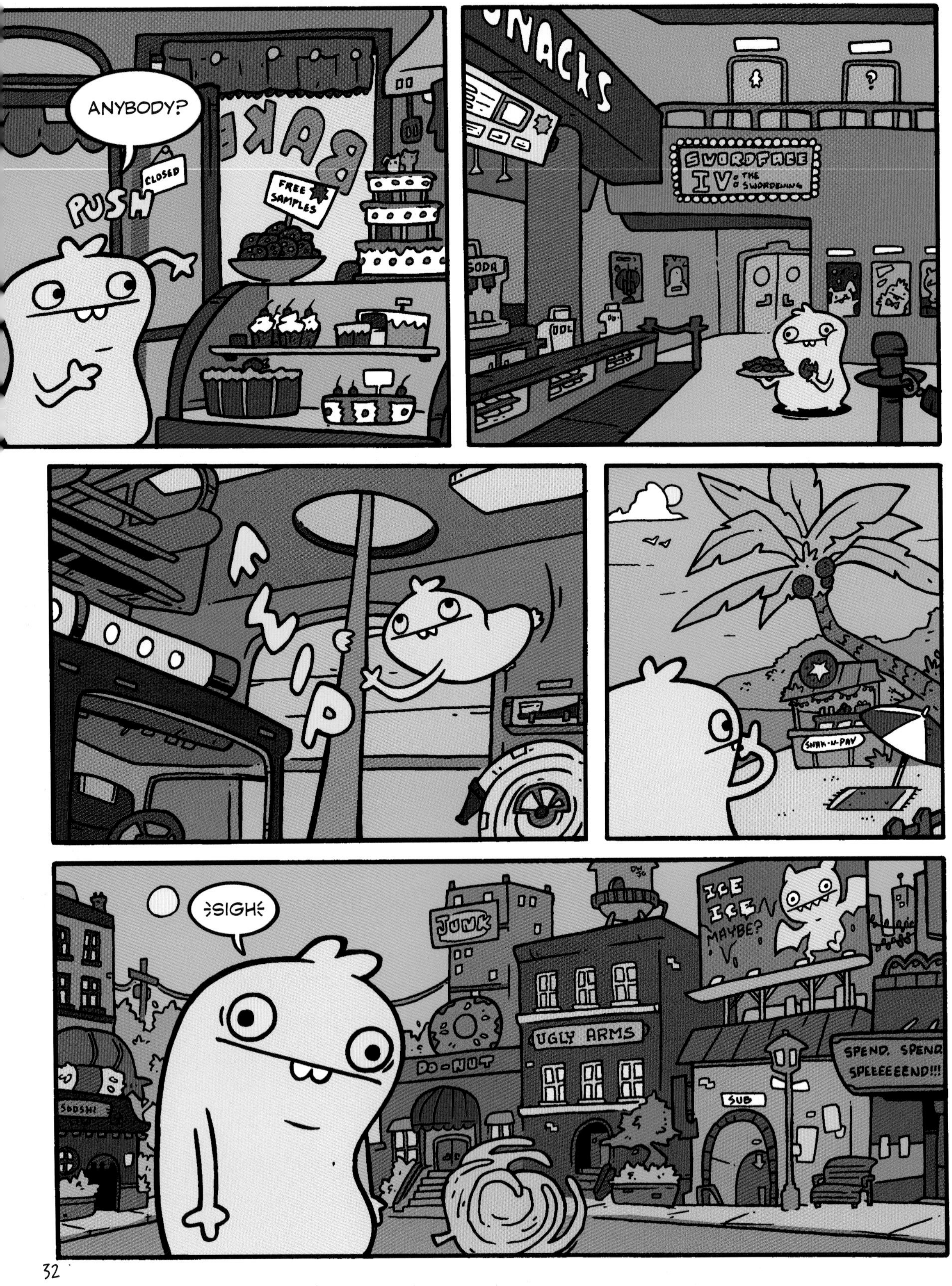
ANYBODY?
CLOSED
PUSH
FREE SAMPLES
NACKS
SWORDFACE
IV: THE SWORDENING
SODA
SNAK-N-PAY
SIGH
JUNK
ICE ICE MAYBE?
UGLY ARMS
DO-NUT
SPEND, SPEND, SPEEEEEEND!!!
SUB
SOOSHI

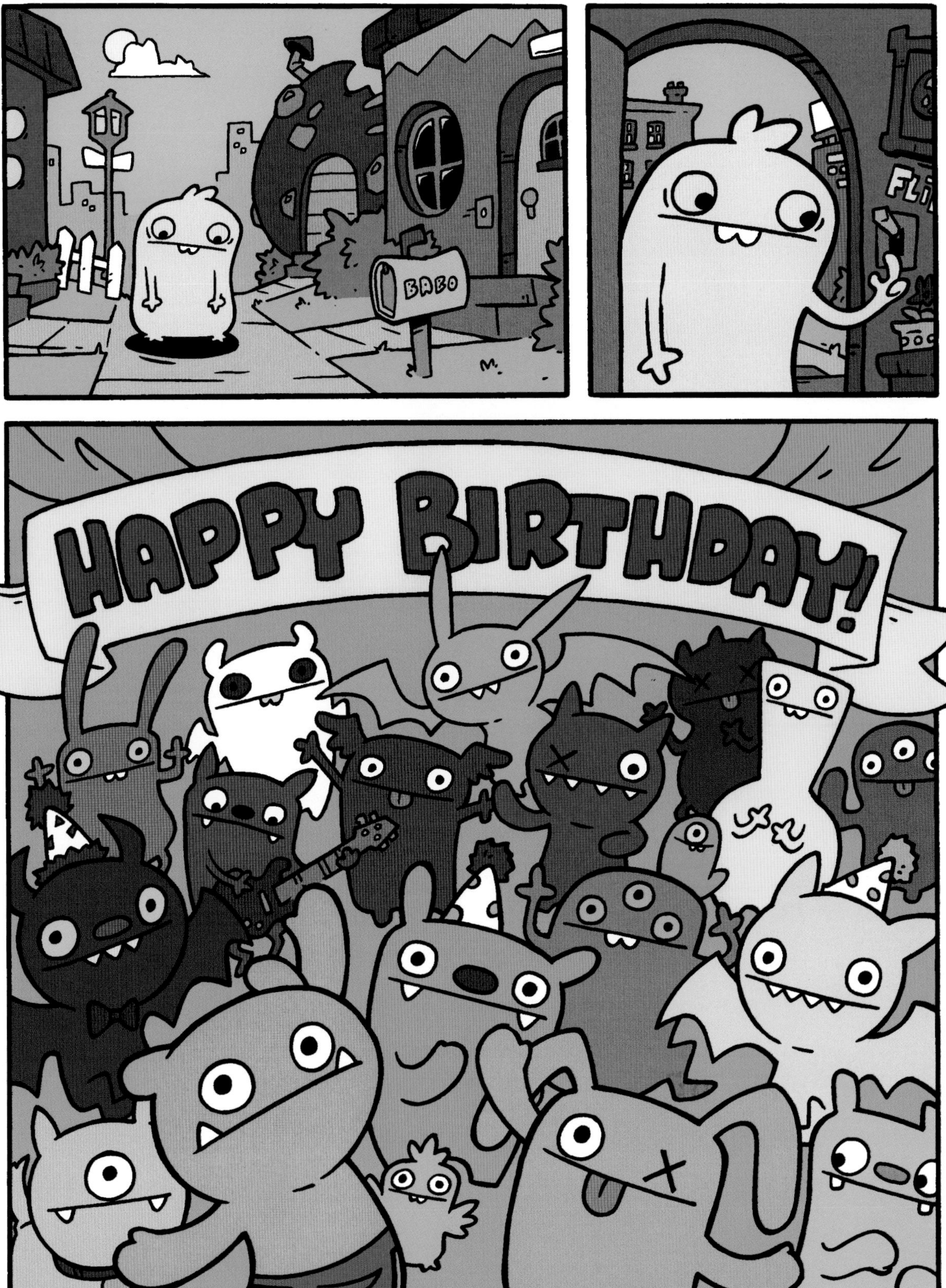
BABO
HAPPY BIRTHDAY!

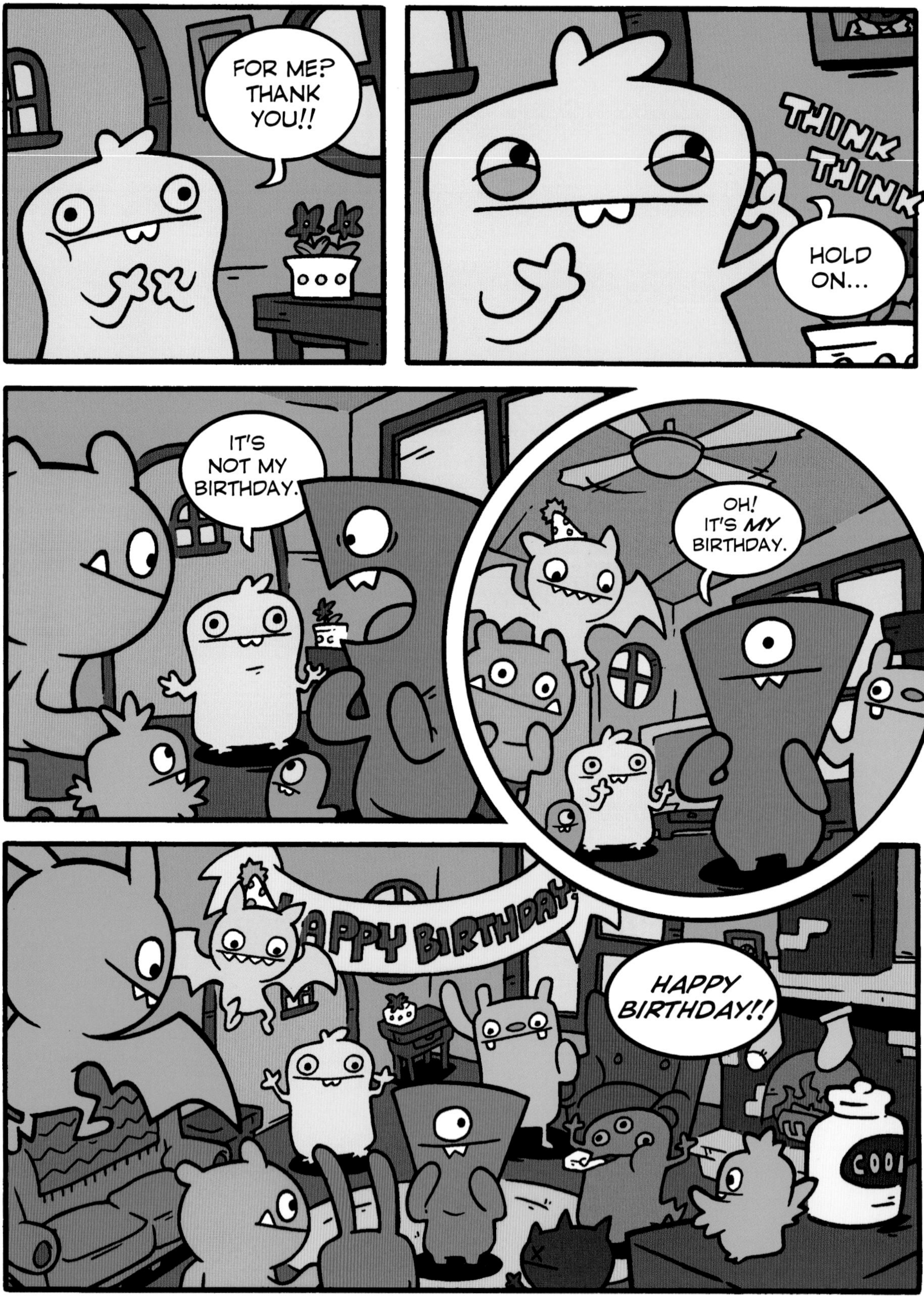
FOR ME? THANK YOU!!
THINK THINK
HOLD ON...
IT'S NOT MY BIRTHDAY.
OH! IT'S *MY* BIRTHDAY.
HAPPY BIRTHDAY!!

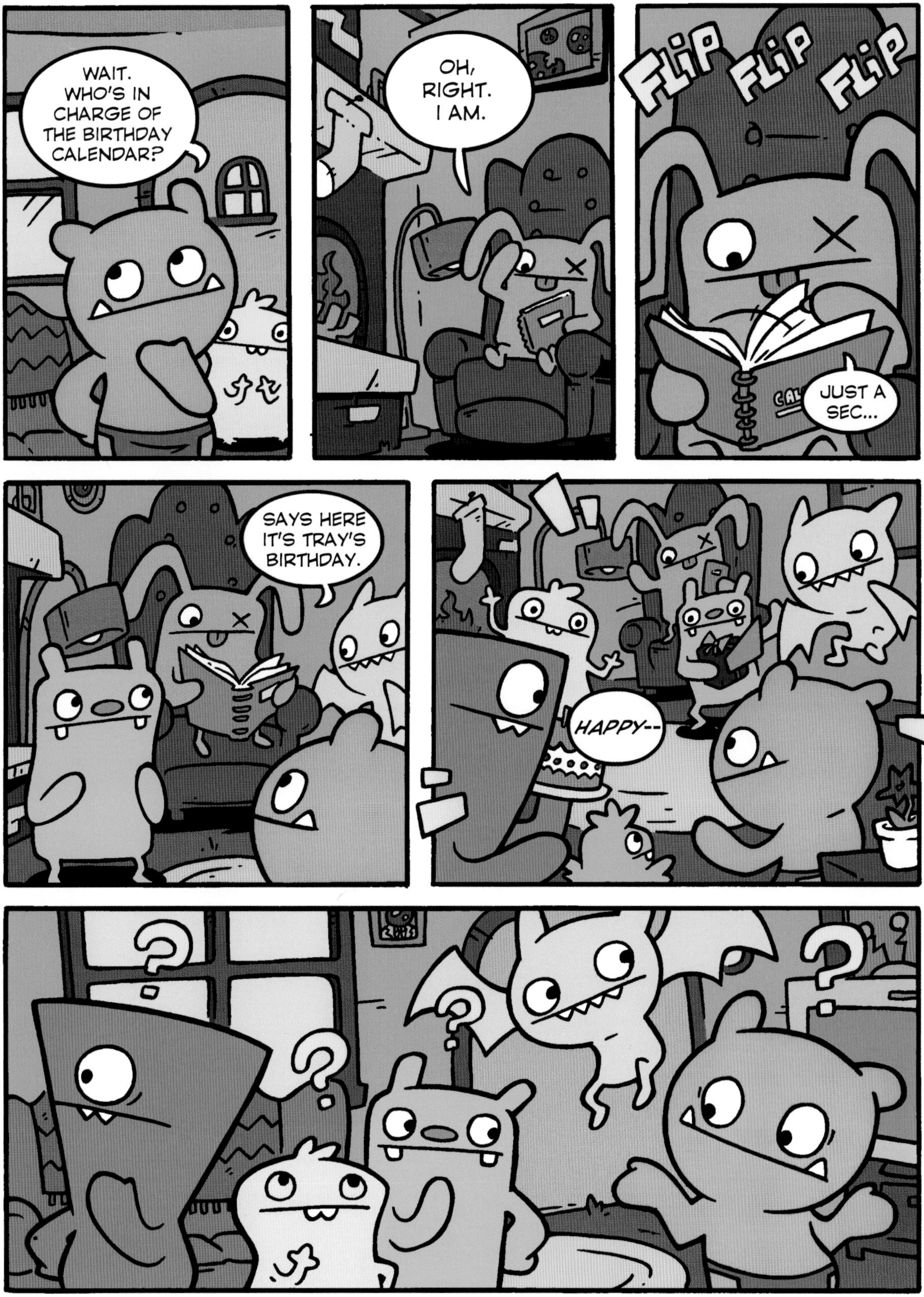
WAIT. WHO'S IN CHARGE OF THE BIRTHDAY CALENDAR?
OH, RIGHT. I AM.
FLIP FLIP FLIP
JUST A SEC...
SAYS HERE IT'S TRAY'S BIRTHDAY.
HAPPY--

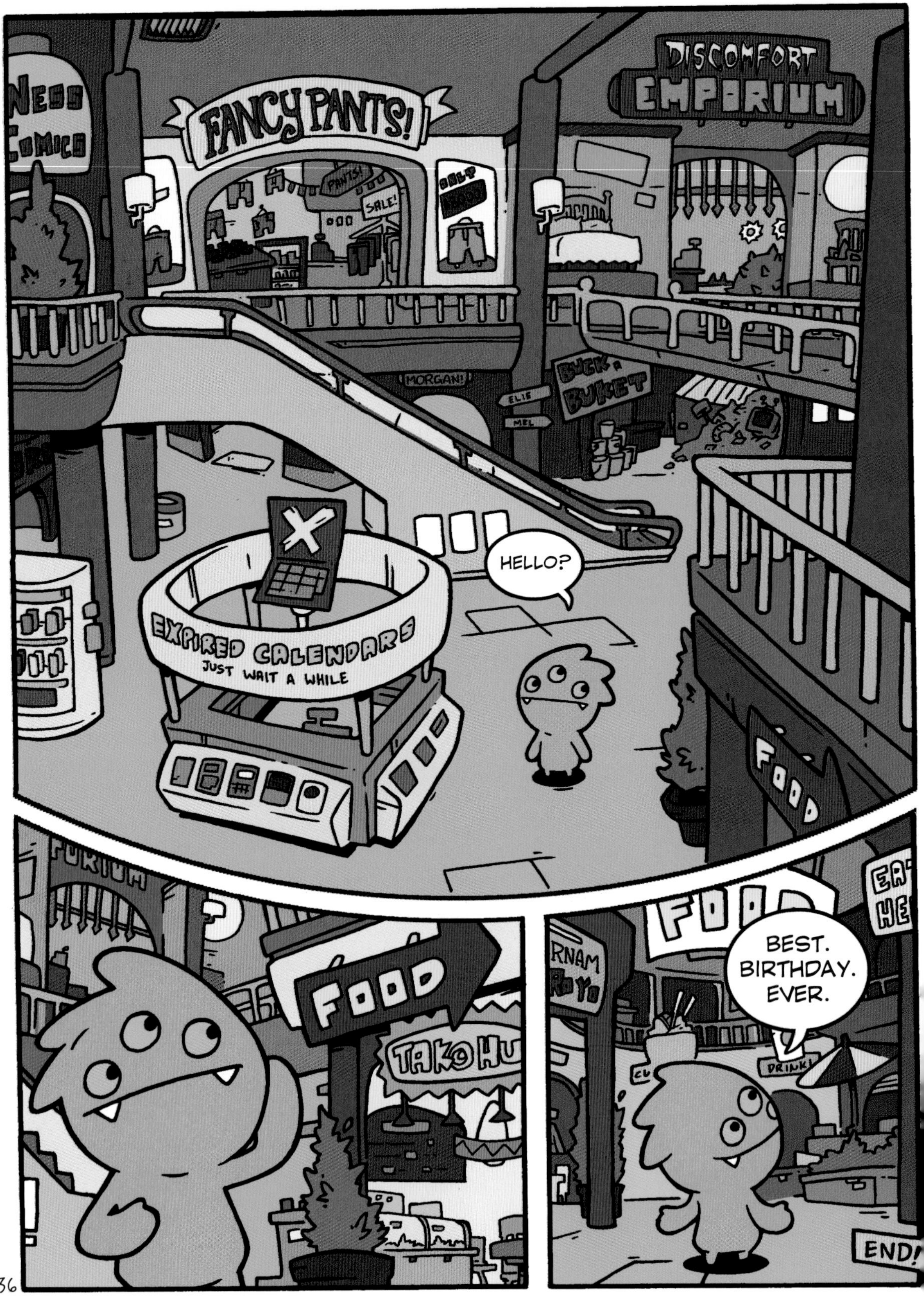
FANCY PANTS!
PANTS!
SALE!
DISCOMFORT EMPIRIUM
MORGAN!
ELIE
MEL
BUCK A BUKET
HELLO?
EXPIRED CALENDARS
JUST WAIT A WHILE
FOOD
FOOD
!
BEST. BIRTHDAY. EVER.
END!

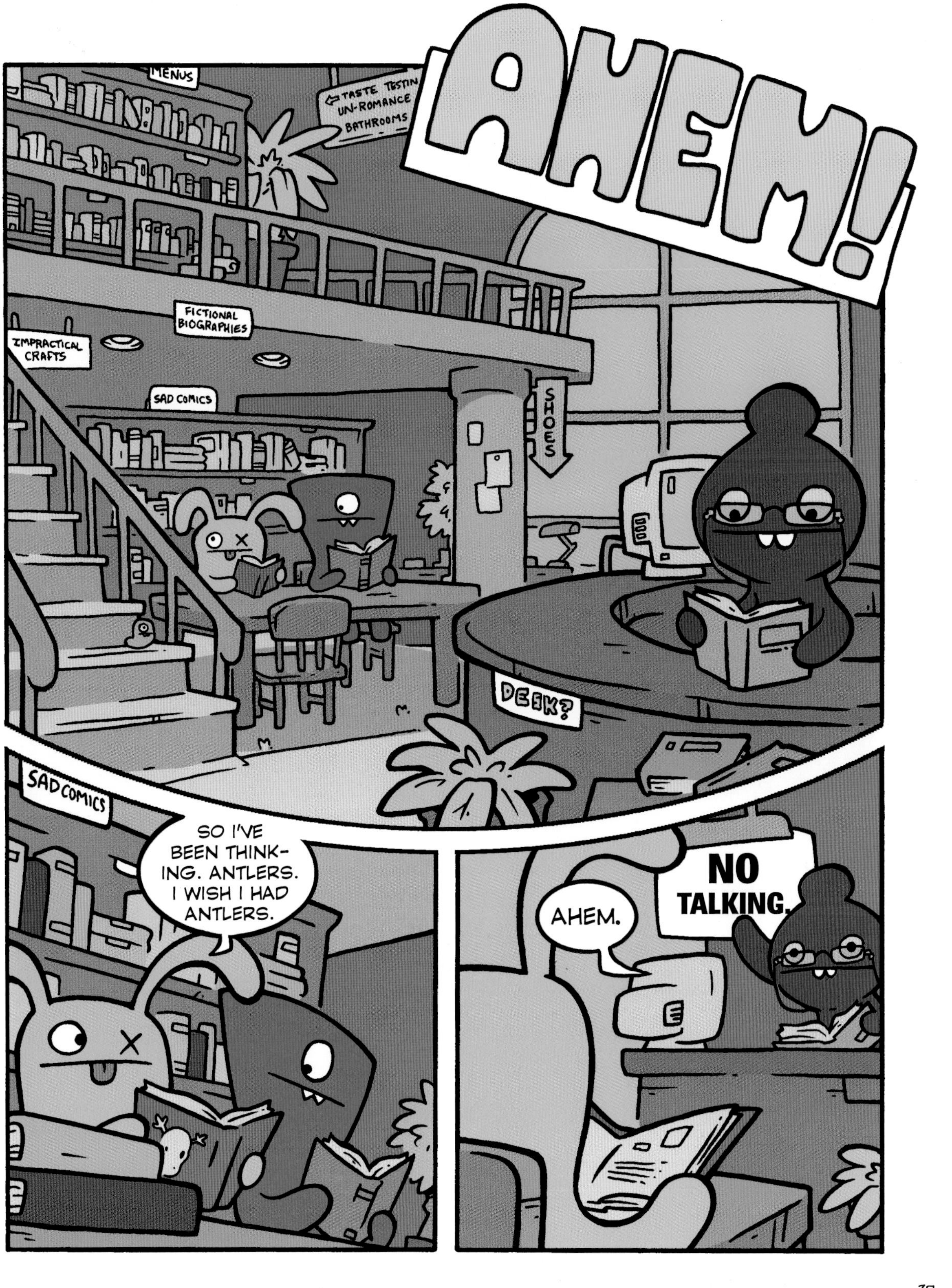
AHEM!
MENUS
TASTE TESTIN
UN-ROMANCE
BATHROOMS
FICTIONAL BIOGRAPHIES
IMPRACTICAL CRAFTS
SAD COMICS
SHOES
DESK?
SAD COMICS
SO I'VE BEEN THINKING. ANTLERS. I WISH I HAD ANTLERS.
AHEM.
NO TALKING.

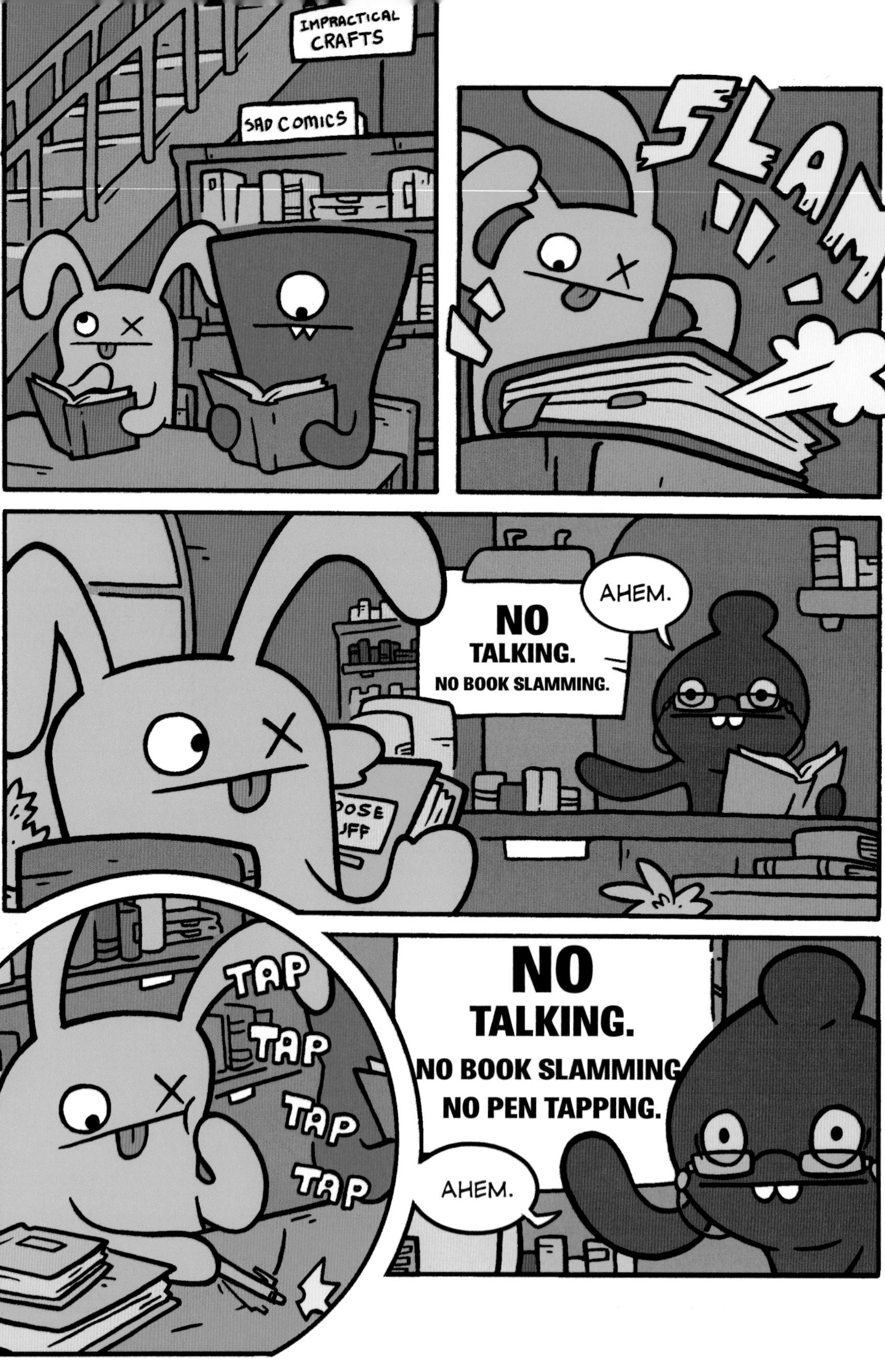
IMPRACTICAL CRAFTS
SAD COMICS
SLAM
NO TALKING. NO BOOK SLAMMING.
AHEM.
TAP
TAP
TAP
TAP
NO TALKING. NO BOOK SLAMMING. NO PEN TAPPING.
AHEM.

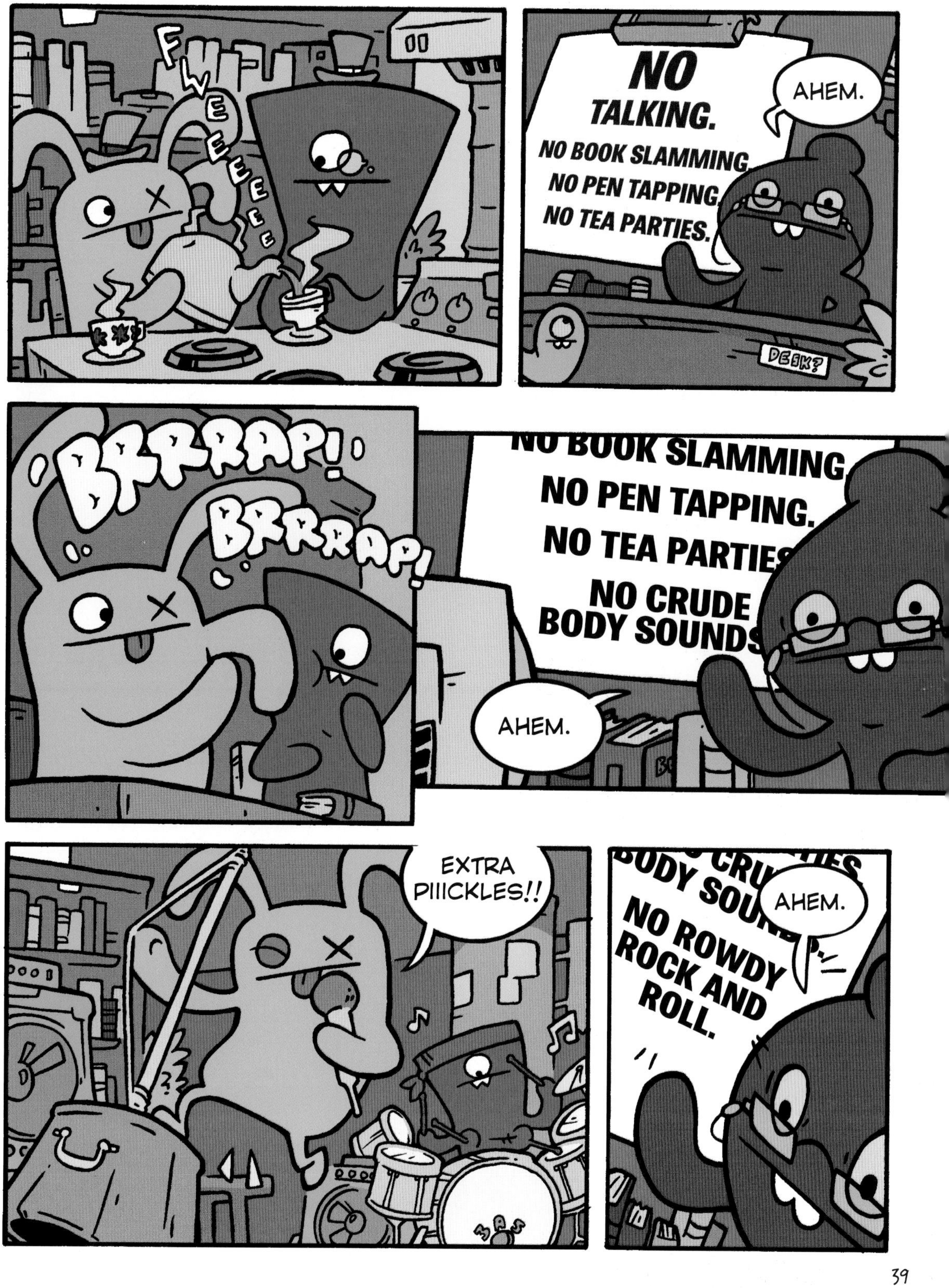
FWEEEEEE
NO TALKING.
NO BOOK SLAMMING.
NO PEN TAPPING.
NO TEA PARTIES.
AHEM.
DESK?
BRRRAP! BRRRAP!
NO BOOK SLAMMING.
NO PEN TAPPING.
NO TEA PARTIES
NO CRUDE BODY SOUNDS
AHEM.
EXTRA PIIICKLES!!
BODY SOUNDS.
NO ROWDY ROCK AND ROLL.
AHEM.

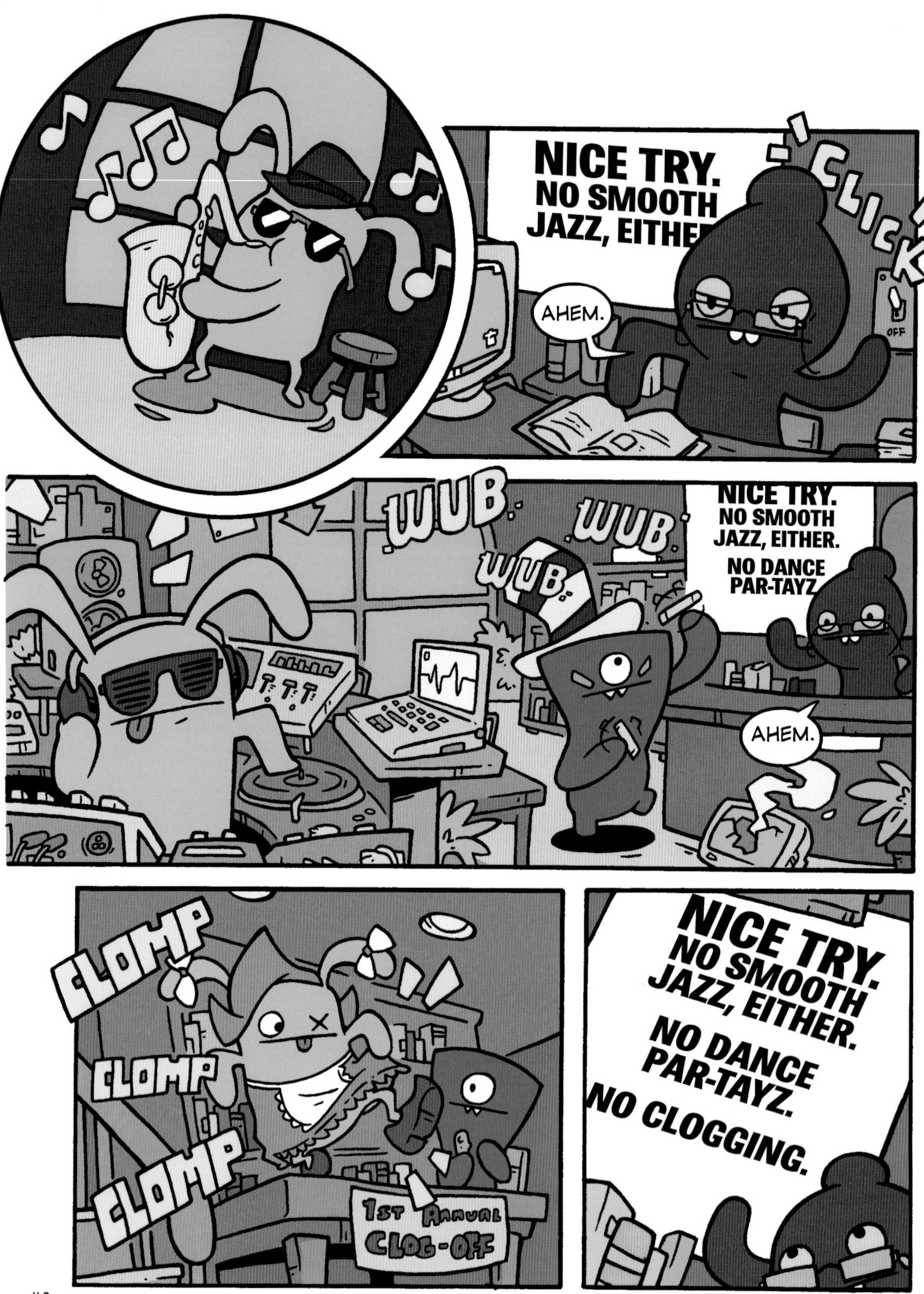

NICE TRY.
NO SMOOTH
JAZZ, EITHER
CLICK
AHEM.
WUB
WUB
WUB
NICE TRY.
NO SMOOTH
JAZZ, EITHER.
NO DANCE
PAR-TAYZ
AHEM.
CLOMP
CLOMP
CLOMP
1ST ANNUAL
CLOG-OFF
NICE TRY.
NO SMOOTH
JAZZ, EITHER.
NO DANCE
PAR-TAYZ.
NO CLOGGING.

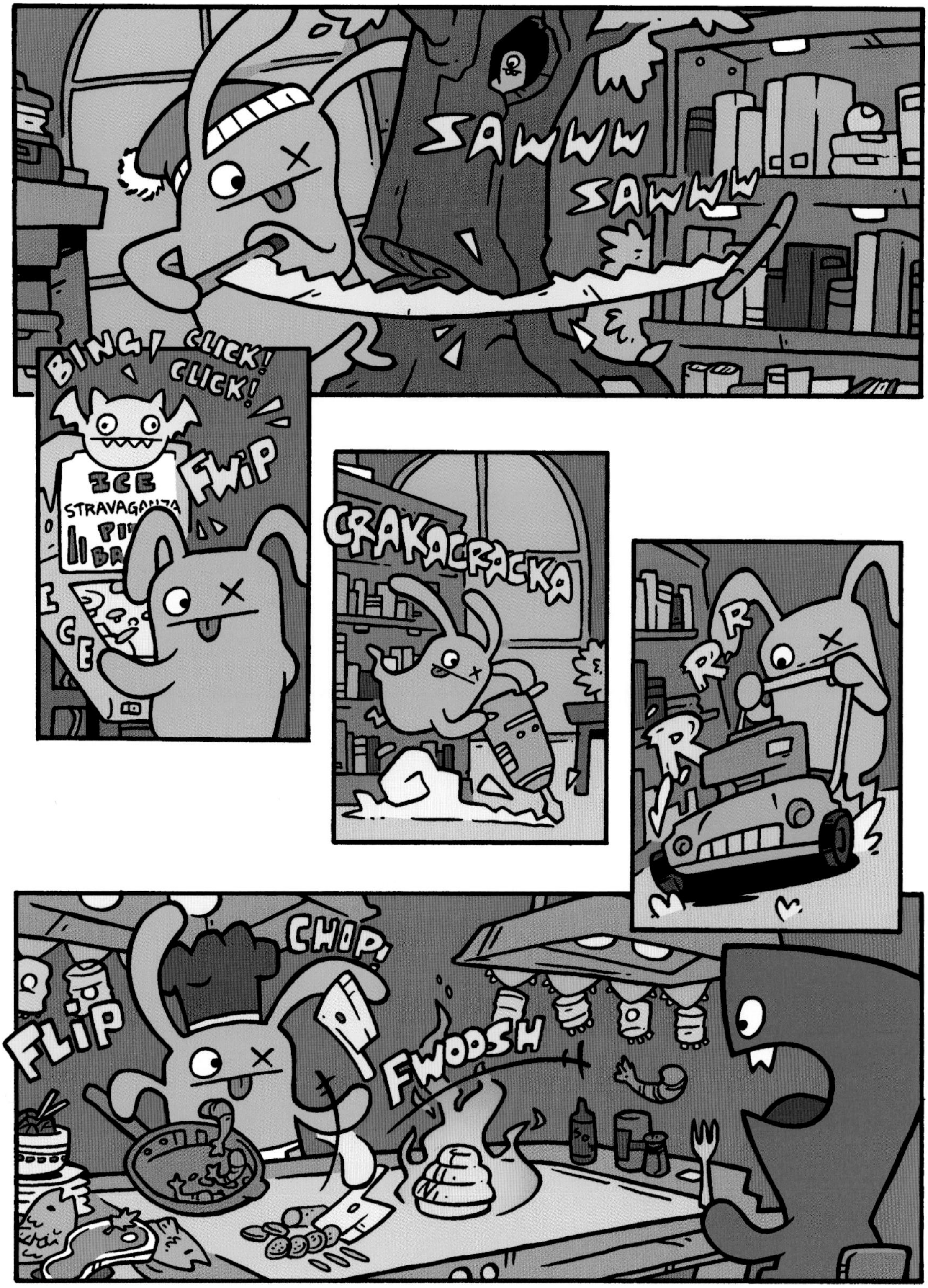
SAWWW
SAWWW
BING!
CLICK! CLICK!
FWIP
ICE
STRAVAGANZA
CRAKACRACKA
RRR
CHIP!
FLIP
FWOOSH

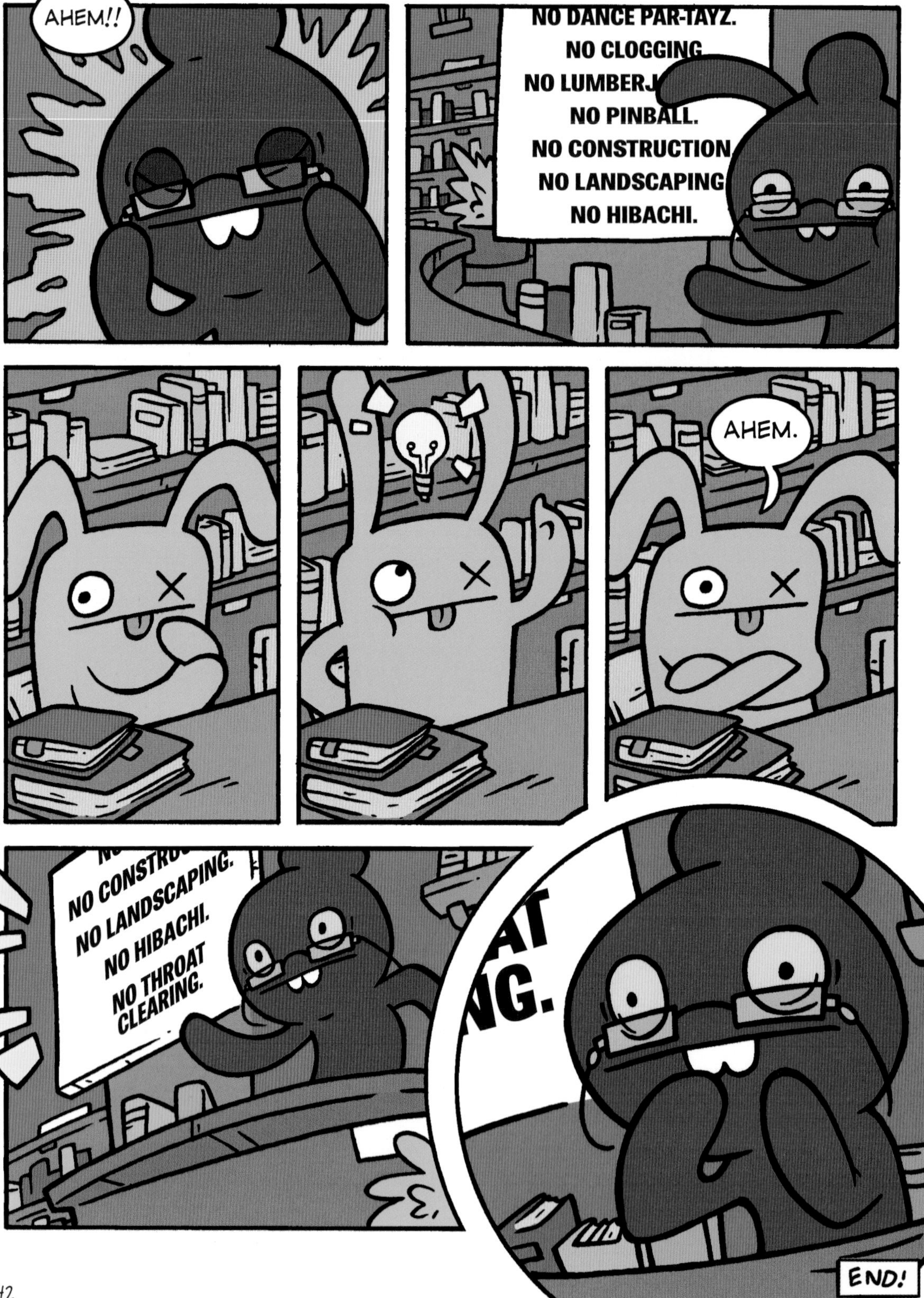
AHEM!!
NO DANCE PAR-TAYZ.
NO CLOGGING.
NO LUMBERJ
NO PINBALL.
NO CONSTRUCTION.
NO LANDSCAPING.
NO HIBACHI.
AHEM.
NO CONSTRU
NO LANDSCAPING.
NO HIBACHI.
NO THROAT
CLEARING.
AT
NG.
END!

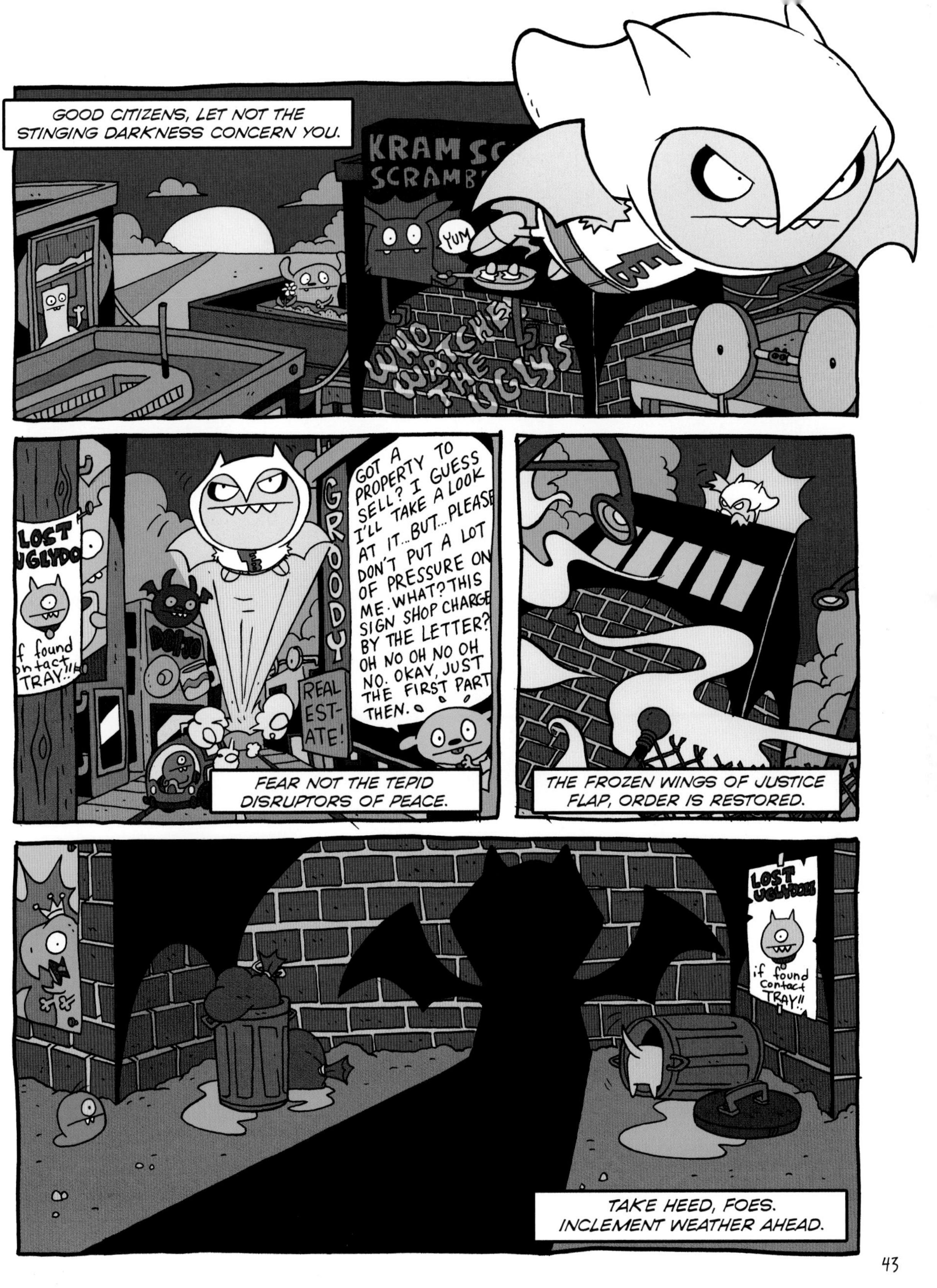
GOOD CITIZENS, LET NOT THE STINGING DARKNESS CONCERN YOU.
KRAM SC
SCRAMB
YUM
WHO WATCHES THE UGLYS
LOST UGLYDO
if found contact TRAY!!
GROODY
GOT A PROPERTY TO SELL? I GUESS I'LL TAKE A LOOK AT IT...BUT...PLEASE DON'T PUT A LOT OF PRESSURE ON ME. WHAT? THIS SIGN SHOP CHARGE BY THE LETTER? OH NO OH NO OH NO. OKAY, JUST THE FIRST PART THEN.
REAL EST-ATE!
FEAR NOT THE TEPID DISRUPTORS OF PEACE.
THE FROZEN WINGS OF JUSTICE FLAP, ORDER IS RESTORED.
LOST UGLYDOLL
if found contact TRAY!!
TAKE HEED, FOES. INCLEMENT WEATHER AHEAD.

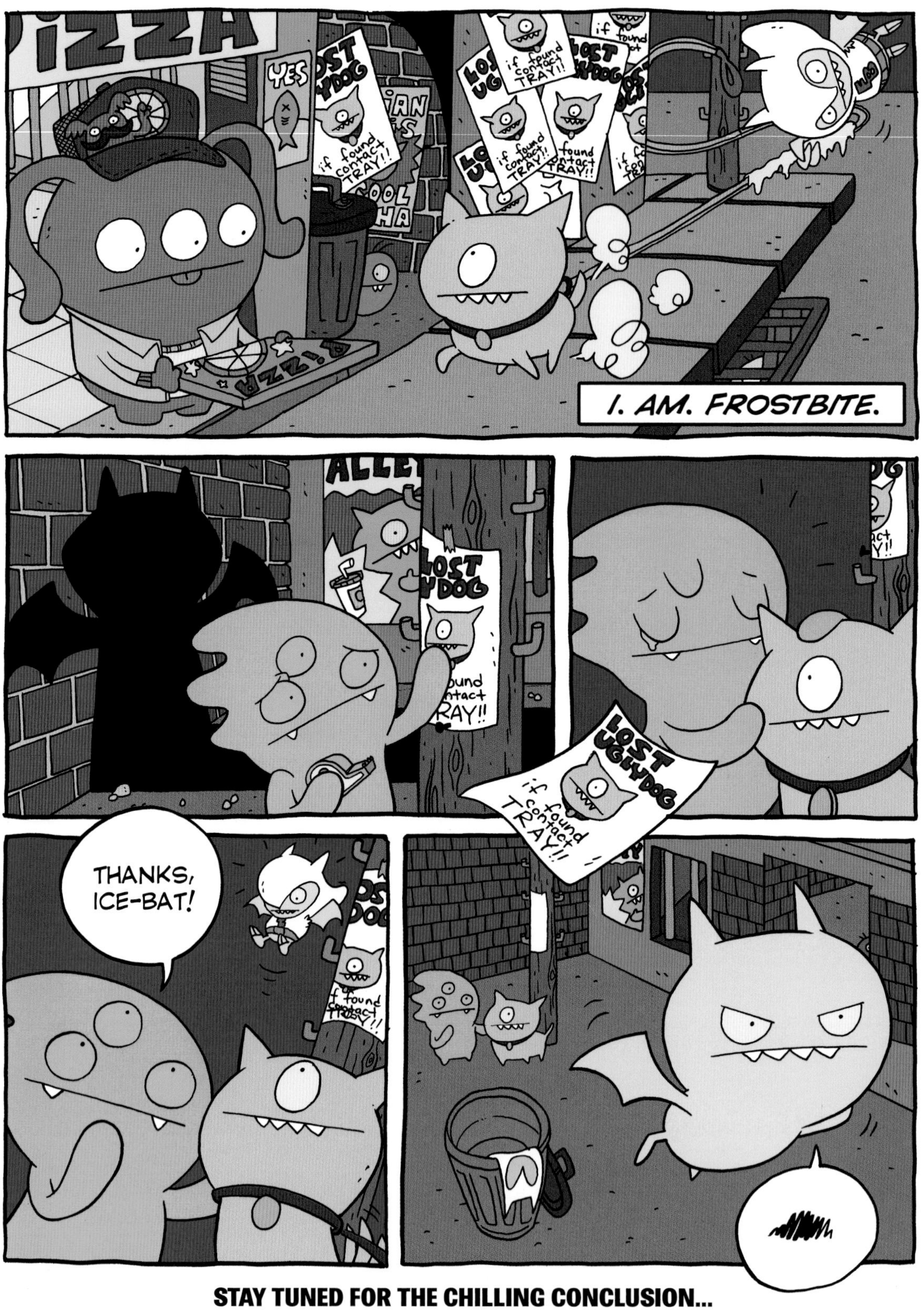
PIZZA
YES
LOST UGLYDOG
if found contact TRAY!!
I. AM. FROSTBITE.
LOST UGLYDOG
if found contact TRAY!!
THANKS, ICE-BAT!

STAY TUNED FOR THE CHILLING CONCLUSION...

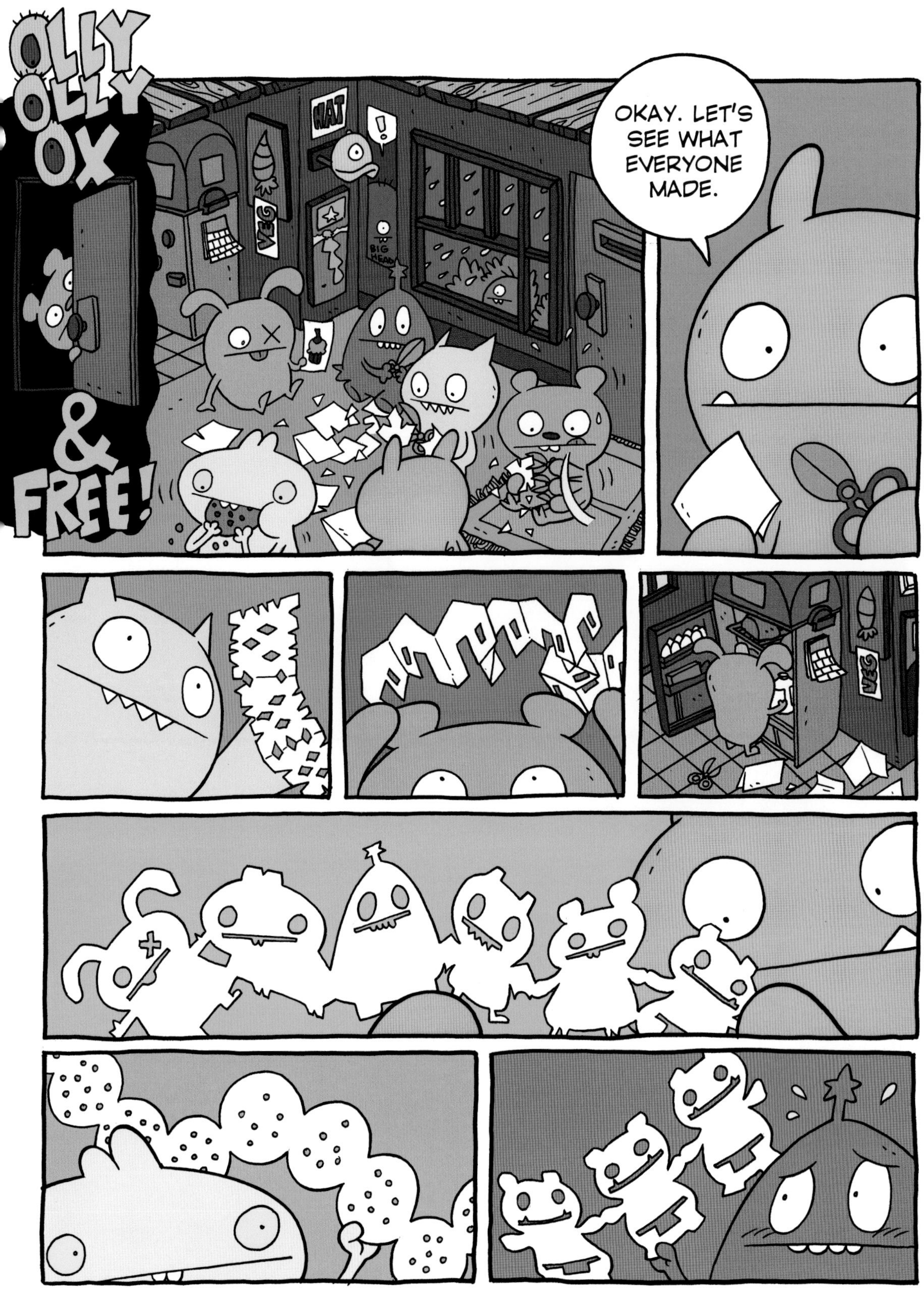
OLLY OLLY OX & FREE!
HAT
VEG
BIG HEAD
OKAY. LET'S SEE WHAT EVERYONE MADE.
VEG

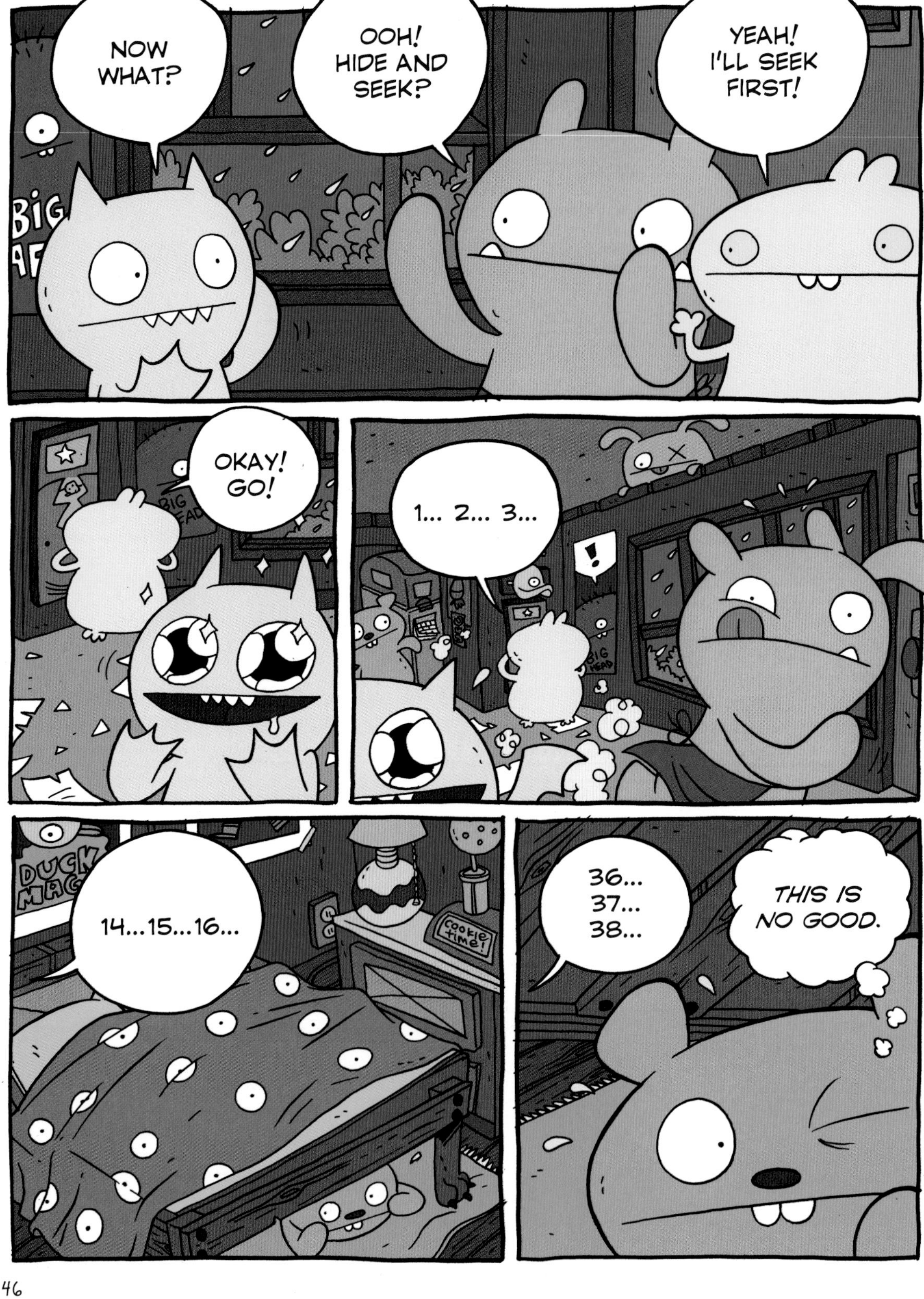
NOW WHAT?
OOH! HIDE AND SEEK?
YEAH! I'LL SEEK FIRST!
OKAY! GO!
1... 2... 3...
14...15...16...
36... 37... 38...
THIS IS NO GOOD.

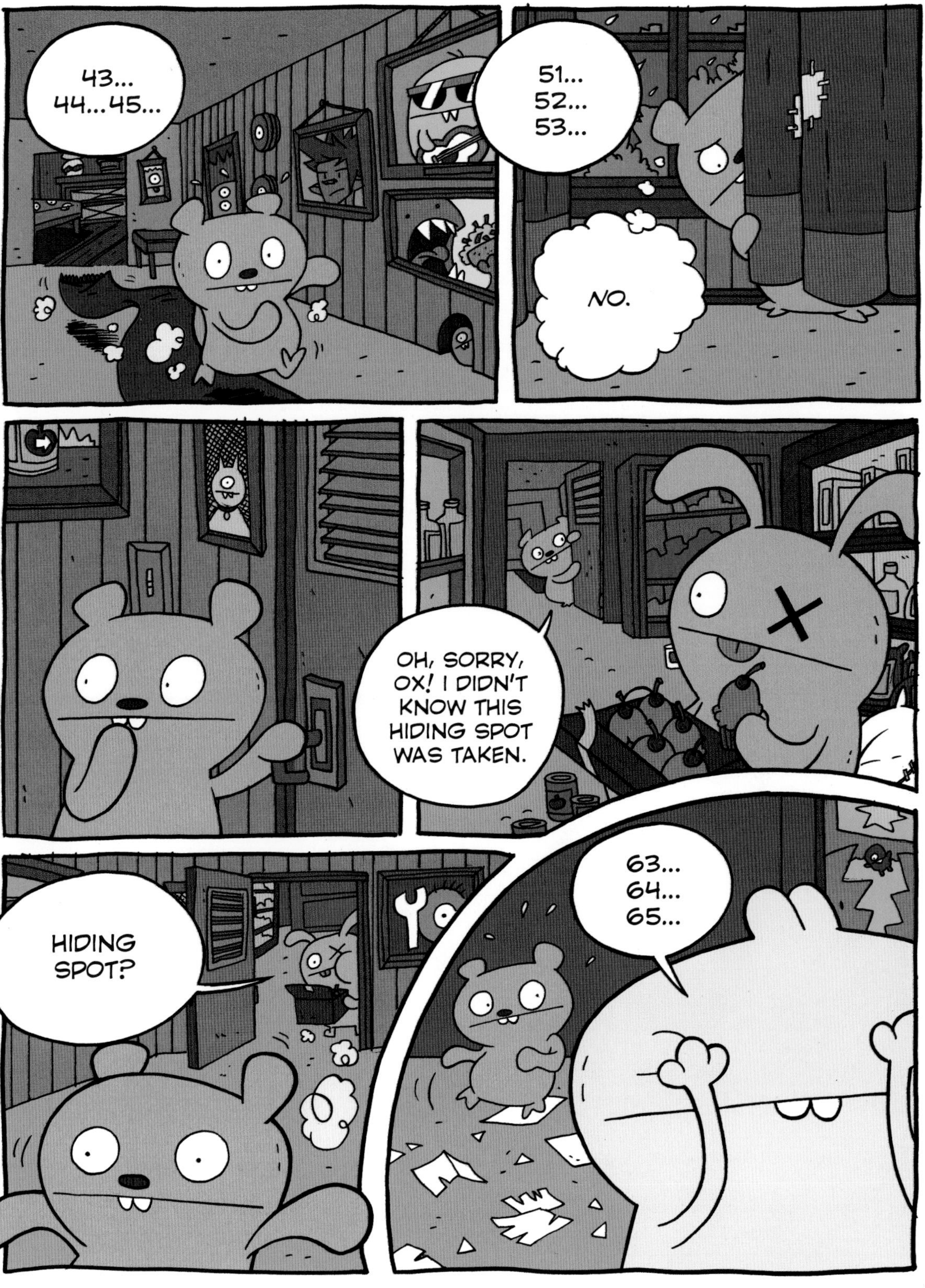
43...
44...45...
51...
52...
53...
NO.
OH, SORRY, OX! I DIDN'T KNOW THIS HIDING SPOT WAS TAKEN.
HIDING SPOT?
63...
64...
65...

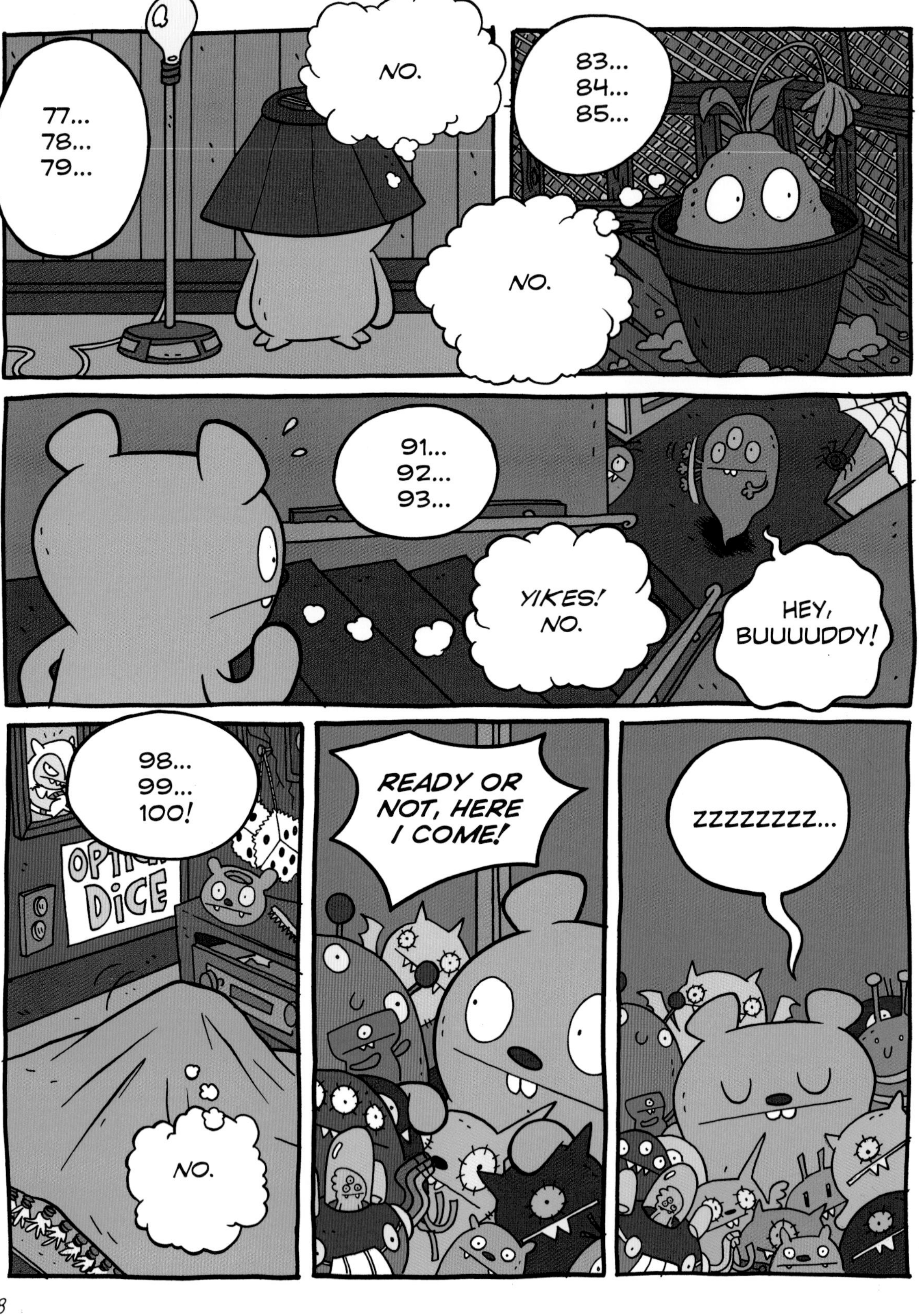
77...
78...
79...
NO.
83...
84...
85...
NO.
91...
92...
93...
YIKES! NO.
HEY, BUUUUDDY!
98...
99...
100!
OPTI
DICE
NO.
READY OR NOT, HERE I COME!
ZZZZZZZZ...

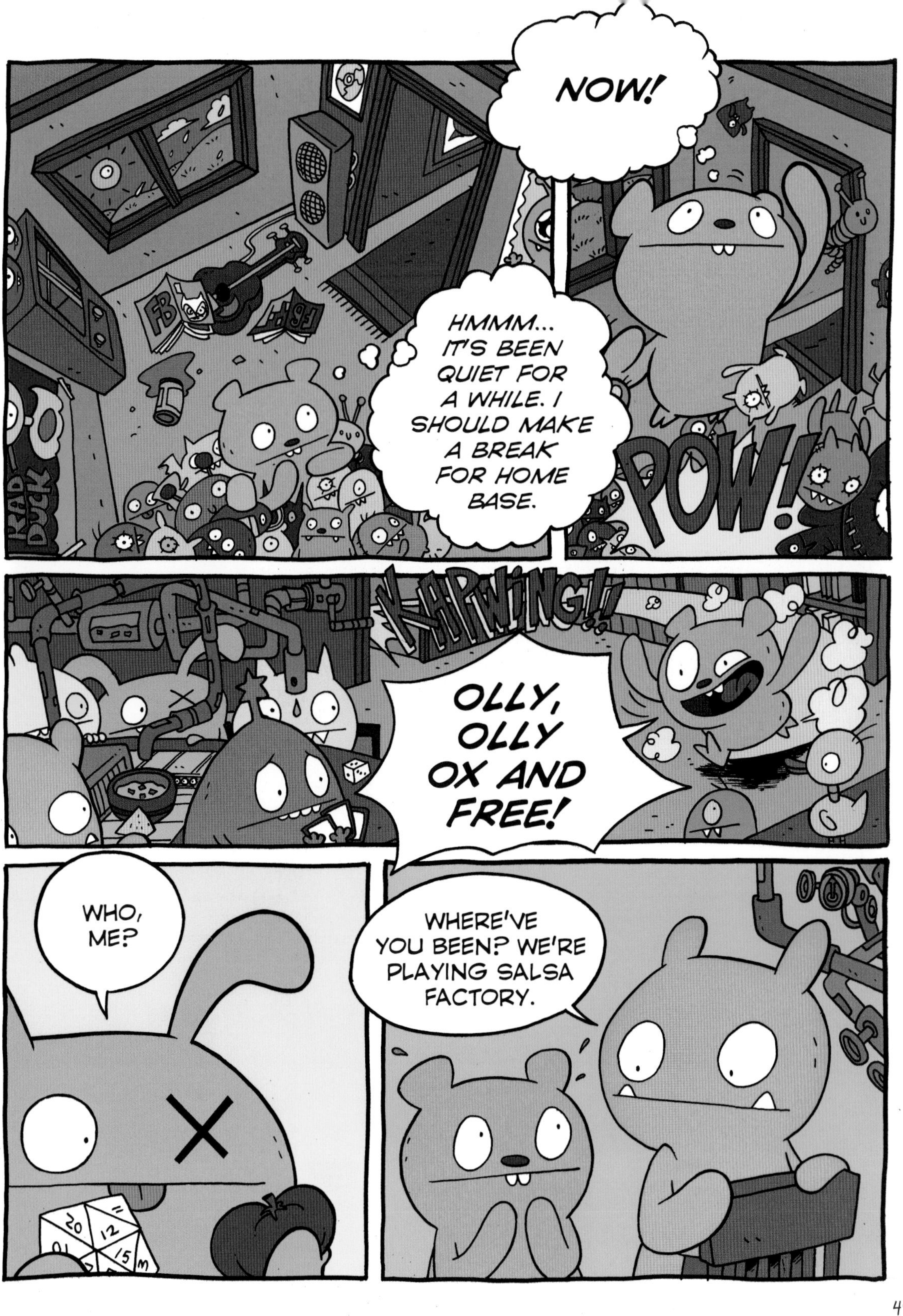
NOW!
HMMM... IT'S BEEN QUIET FOR A WHILE. I SHOULD MAKE A BREAK FOR HOME BASE.
POW!
RAD DUCK
KAPWING!!
OLLY, OLLY OX AND FREE!
WHO, ME?
WHERE'VE YOU BEEN? WE'RE PLAYING SALSA FACTORY.

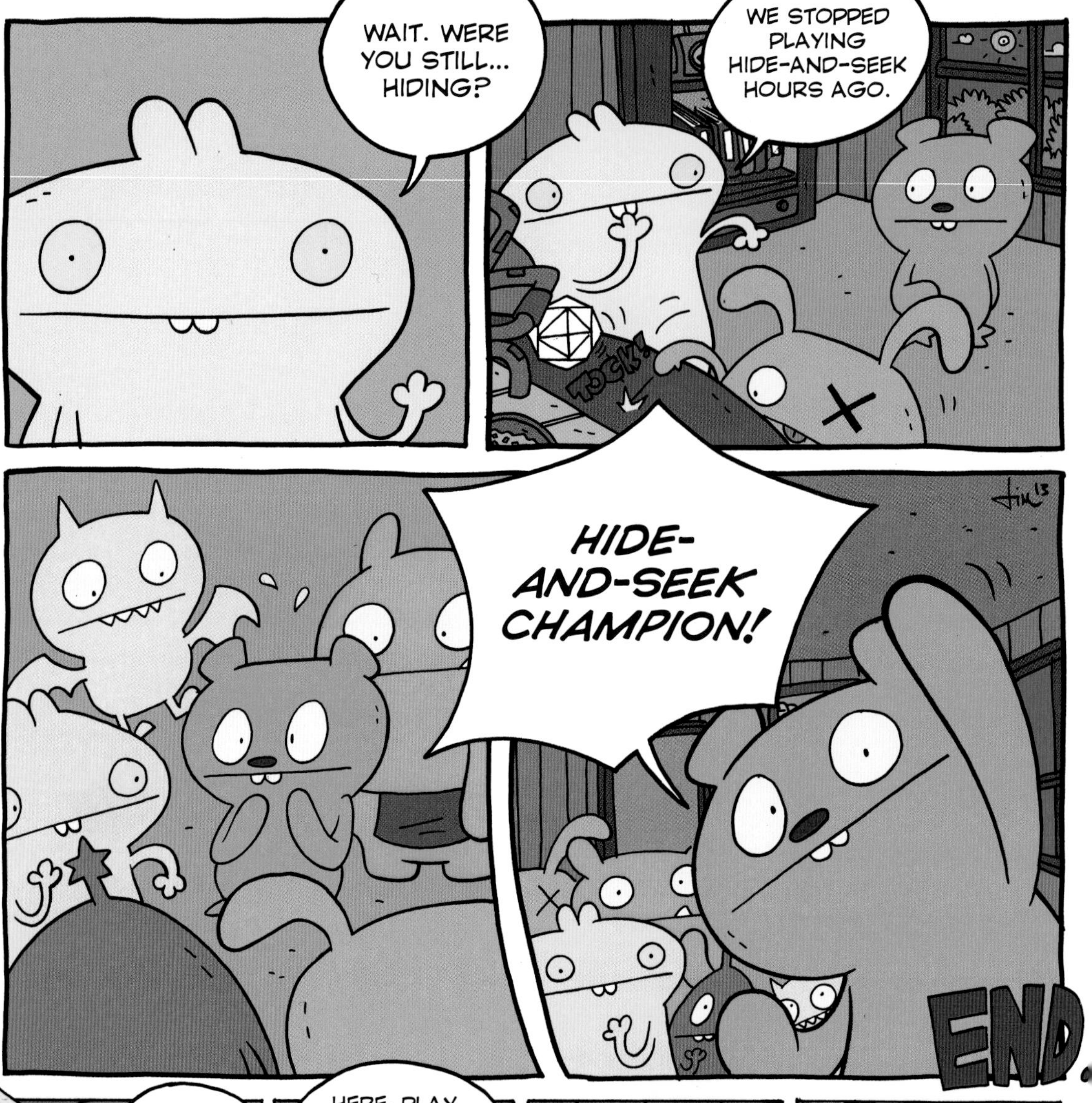
WAIT. WERE YOU STILL... HIDING?
WE STOPPED PLAYING HIDE-AND-SEEK HOURS AGO.
TOCK!
HIDE-AND-SEEK CHAMPION!
END.

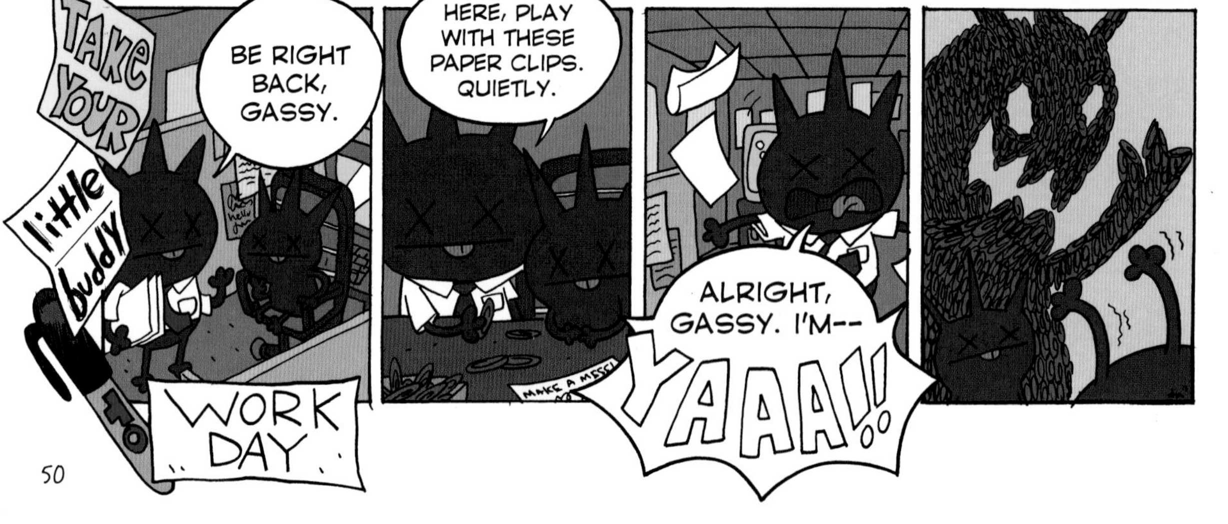
TAKE YOUR little buddy
WORK DAY
BE RIGHT BACK, GASSY.
HERE, PLAY WITH THESE PAPER CLIPS. QUIETLY.
ALRIGHT, GASSY. I'M--
YAAA!!

IS YOUR INNER SELF LACKING?

HIRE AN OUTER SELF

Does ANY or ALL of the following sound like YOU?
It's okay. Be honest. We're here to help.

DO YOU LACK CONFIDENCE?

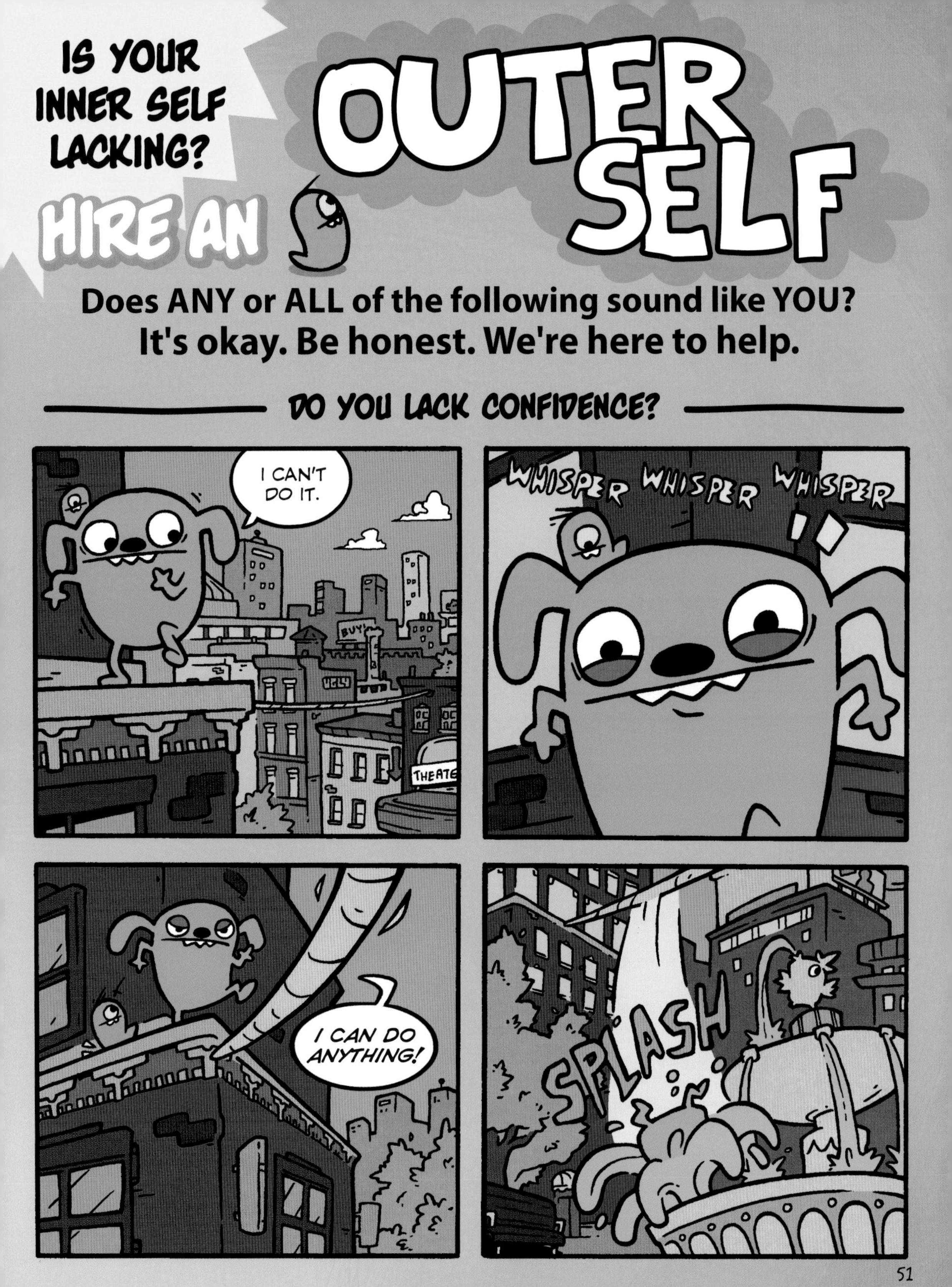
I CAN'T DO IT.
BUY!
THEATE
WHISPER WHISPER WHISPER
I CAN DO ANYTHING!
SPLASH

DO YOU HAVE TROUBLE TELLING RIGHT FROM WRONG?

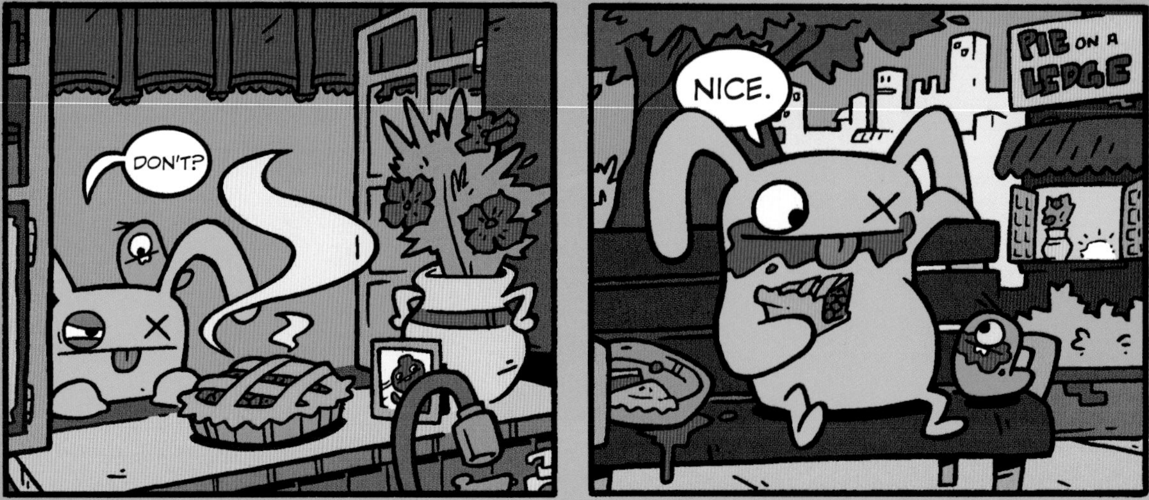
DON'T?
PIE ON A LEDGE
NICE.

DO YOU HAVE A TERRIBLE SENSE OF DIRECTION?

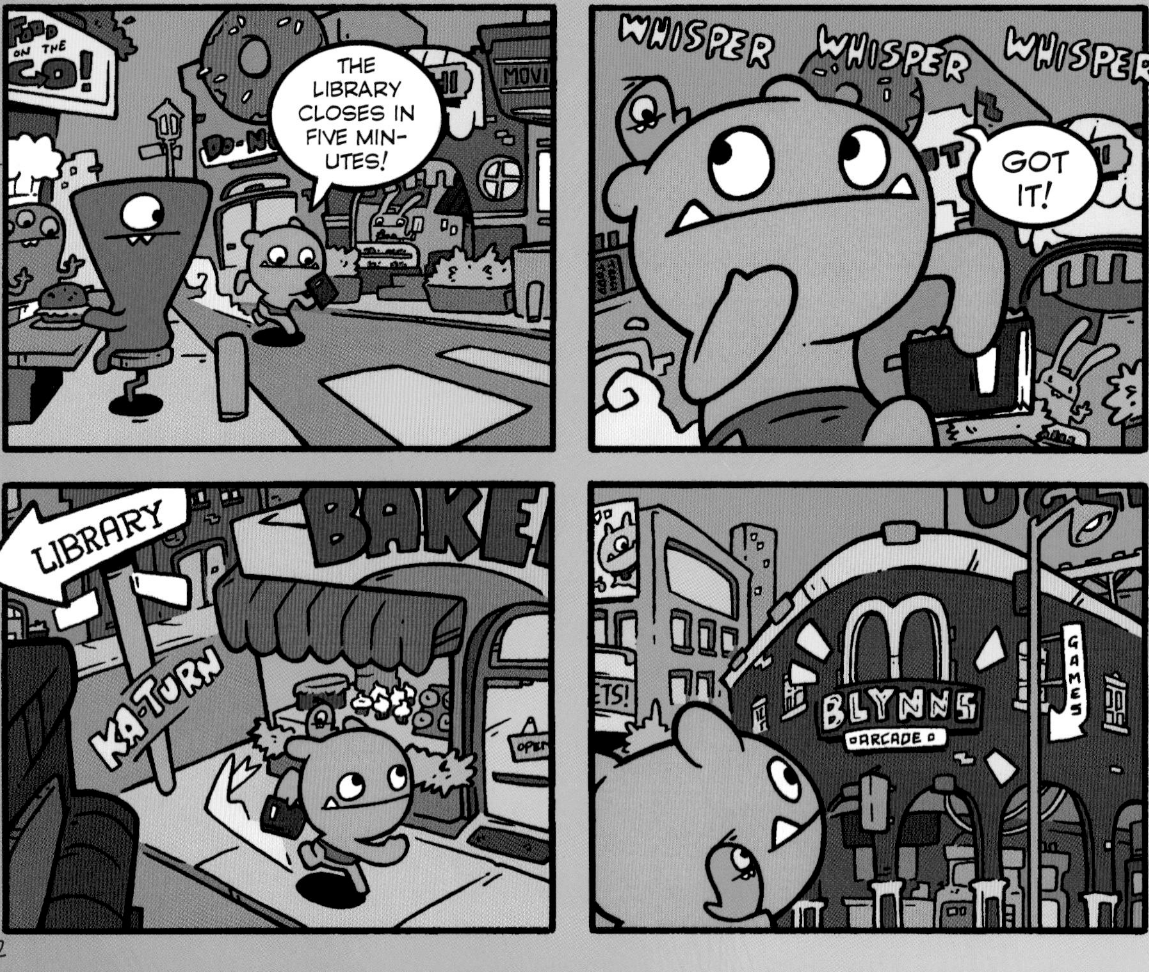
THE LIBRARY CLOSES IN FIVE MIN-UTES!
WHISPER
WHISPER
WHISPER
GOT IT!
LIBRARY
KA-TURN
BLYNNS
ARCADE
GAMES

DO YOU HAVE A BAD MEMORY?

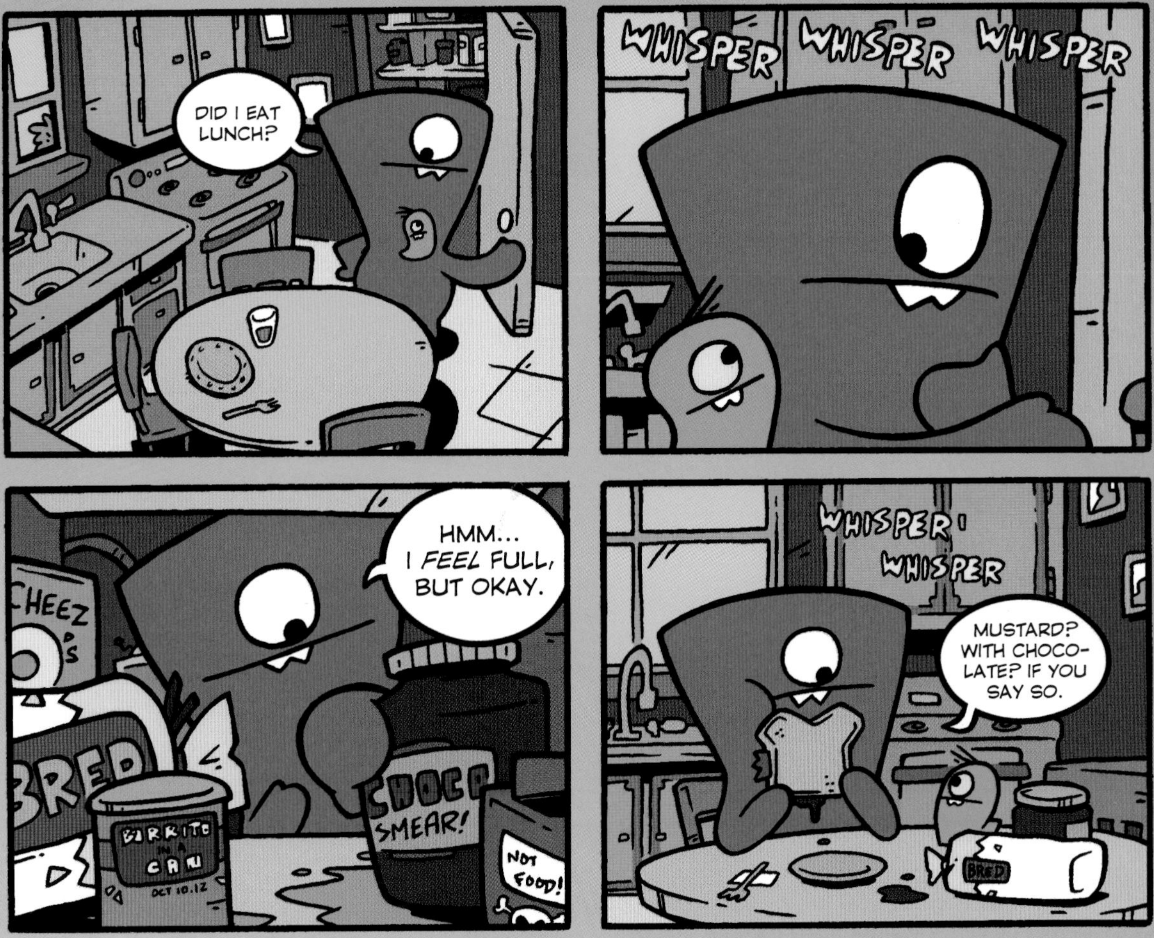

DID I EAT LUNCH?
WHISPER WHISPER WHISPER
CHEEZ
BRED
HMM... I *FEEL* FULL, BUT OKAY.
BURRITO IN A CAN
OCT 10.12
CHOCO SMEAR!
NOT FOOD!
WHISPER WHISPER
MUSTARD? WITH CHOCOLATE? IF YOU SAY SO.
BRED

DO YOU HAVE A HARD TIME PAYING ATTENTION?

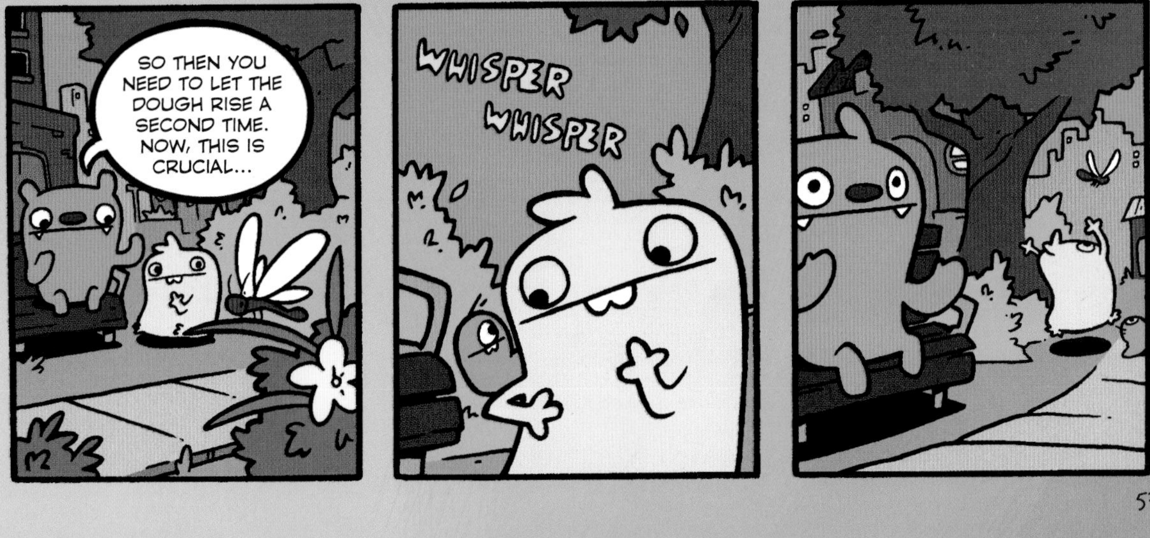

SO THEN YOU NEED TO LET THE DOUGH RISE A SECOND TIME. NOW, THIS IS CRUCIAL...
WHISPER WHISPER

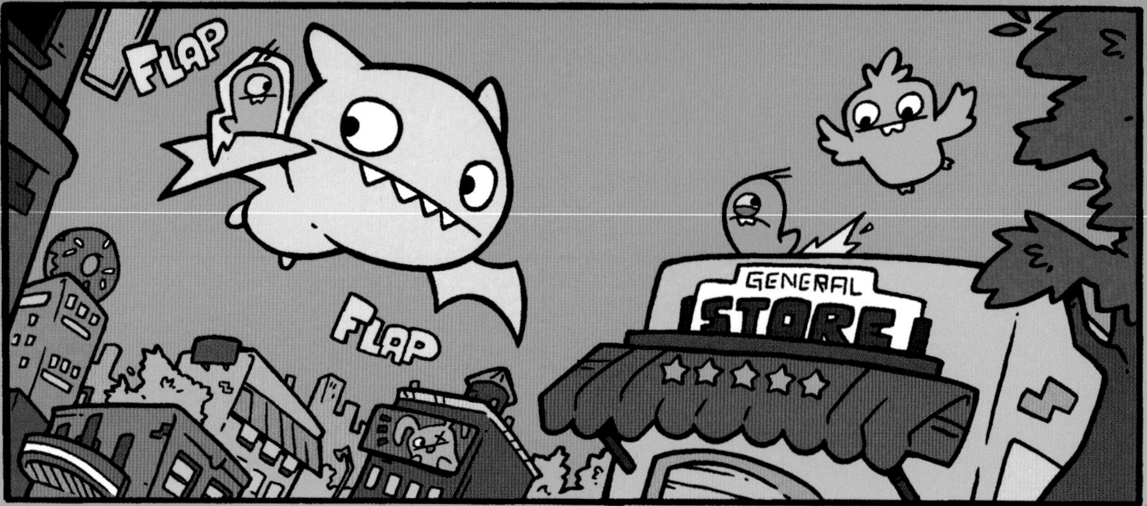

FLAP
FLAP
GENERAL STORE

SERVICES NOT AVAILABLE TO ALL.

Please inquire for details.

OUTER SELF INDUSTRIES can pair you with a wise, insightful, infallible Uglyworm to guide you through the challenging moments in your life.

Give us your trust. Give us all of your trust. Thaaaaat's it.

Call **1(X98) 46@-9W13** or find us on the webs at **uww.outerself:UG**

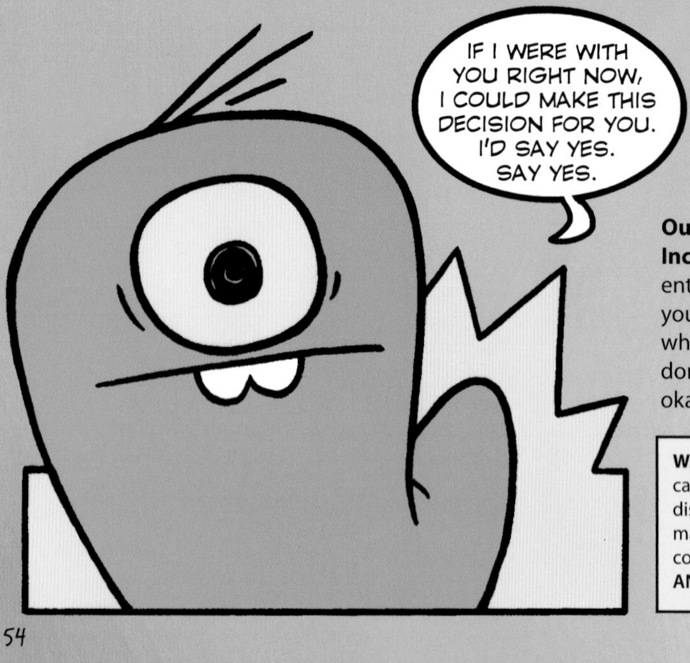

IF I WERE WITH YOU RIGHT NOW, I COULD MAKE THIS DECISION FOR YOU. I'D SAY YES. SAY YES.

Outer Self Industries and **Uglyworm Services, Inc.** are registered corporate such-and-suches. By entering into a contract with said consortiums, you agree to take care of your Uglyworm and do whatever he or she says without question. Hey, don't worry about it. Everything is going to be okay. We're in this together.

WARNING: Extended contact with Uglyworms can cause neck crinks and shoulder ouchies. In case of discomfort, ask your Uglyworm for directions to a chair massage store. He or she will take care of the rest. Also, could we go see a couple of movies? I'd really like that, **AND SO WOULD YOU.**

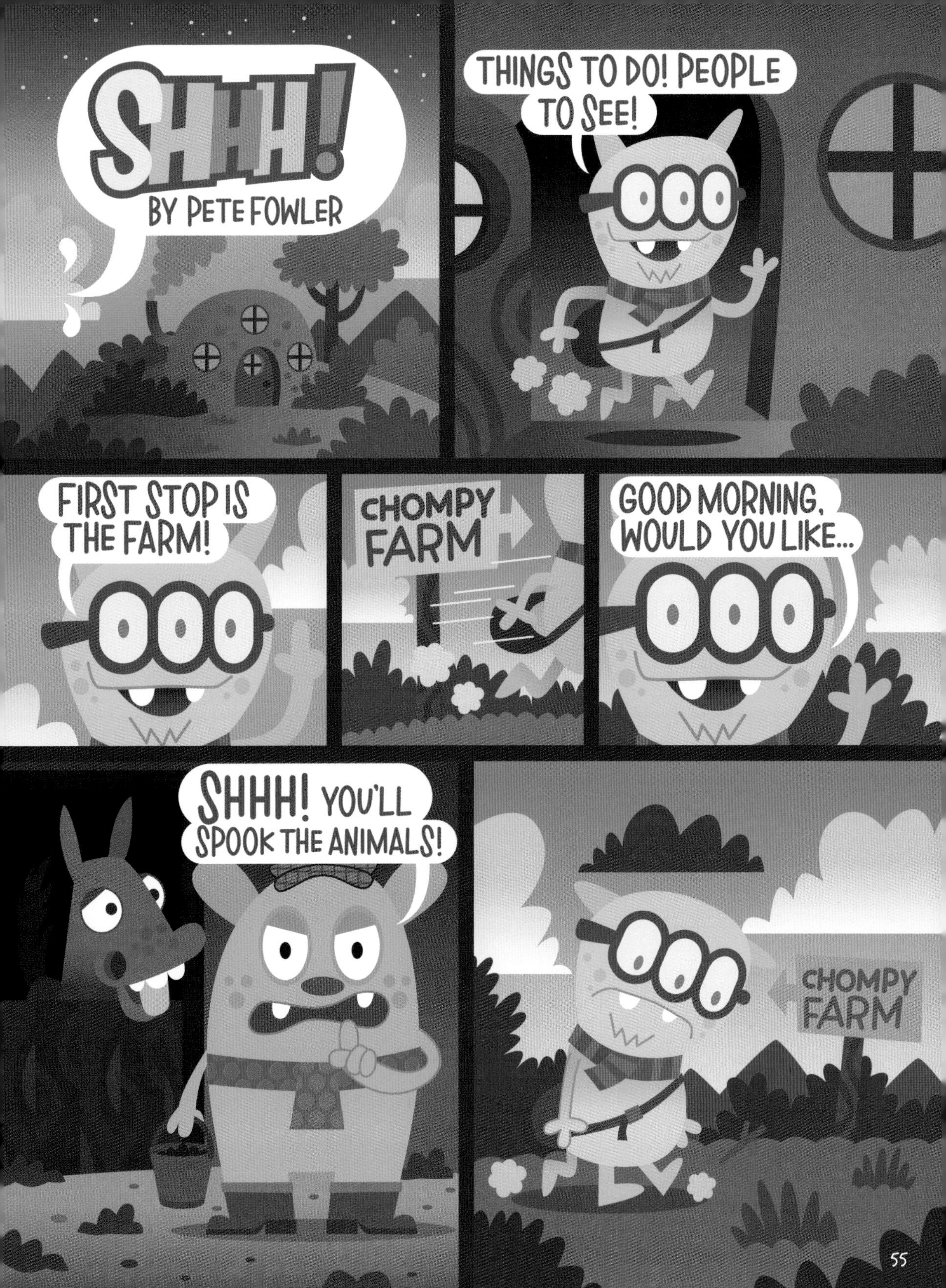
SHHH!
BY PETE FOWLER
THINGS TO DO! PEOPLE TO SEE!
FIRST STOP IS THE FARM!
CHOMPY FARM
GOOD MORNING, WOULD YOU LIKE...
SHHH! YOU'LL SPOOK THE ANIMALS!
CHOMPY FARM

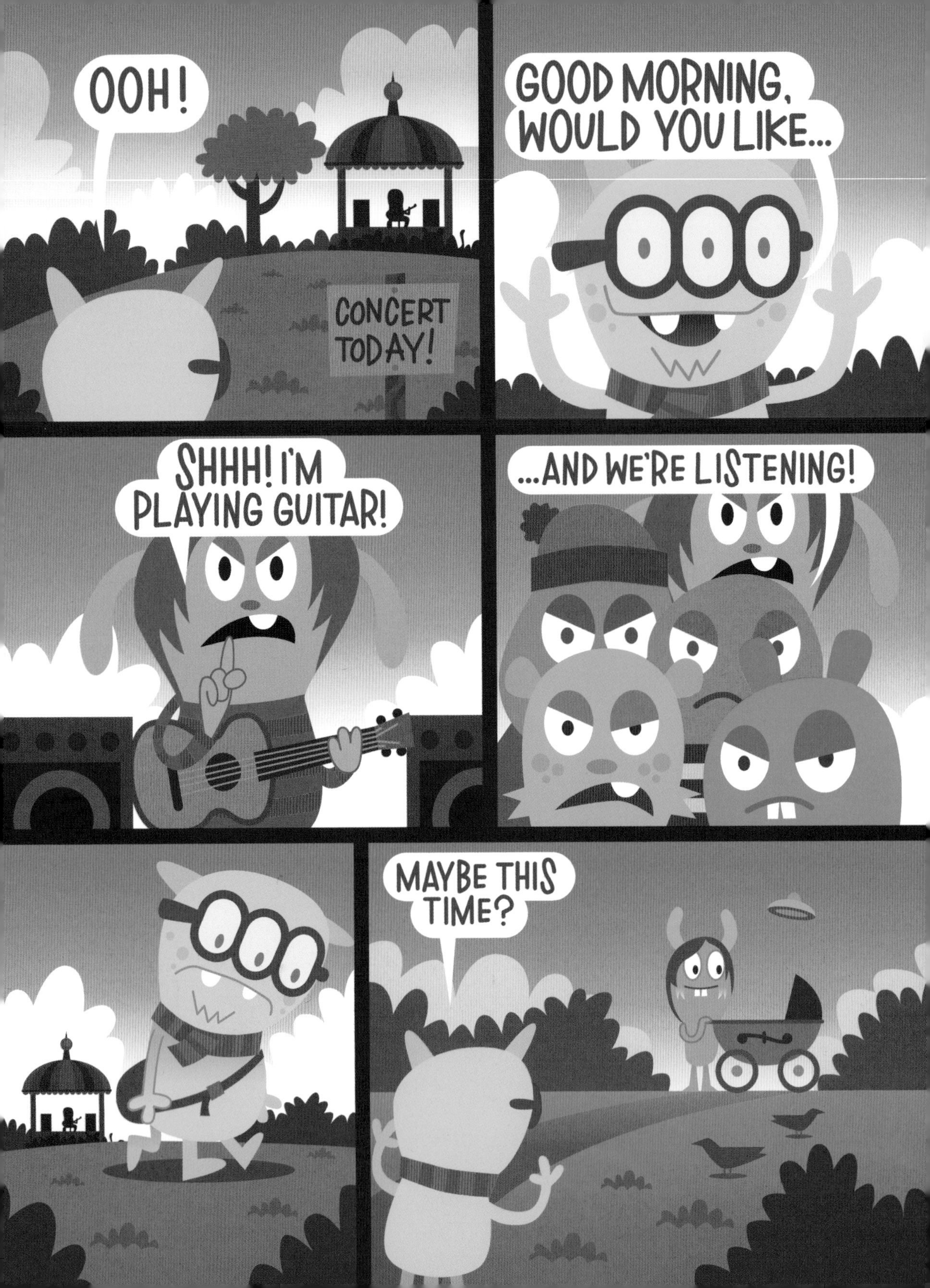
OOH!
CONCERT TODAY!
GOOD MORNING, WOULD YOU LIKE...
SHHH! I'M PLAYING GUITAR!
...AND WE'RE LISTENING!
MAYBE THIS TIME?

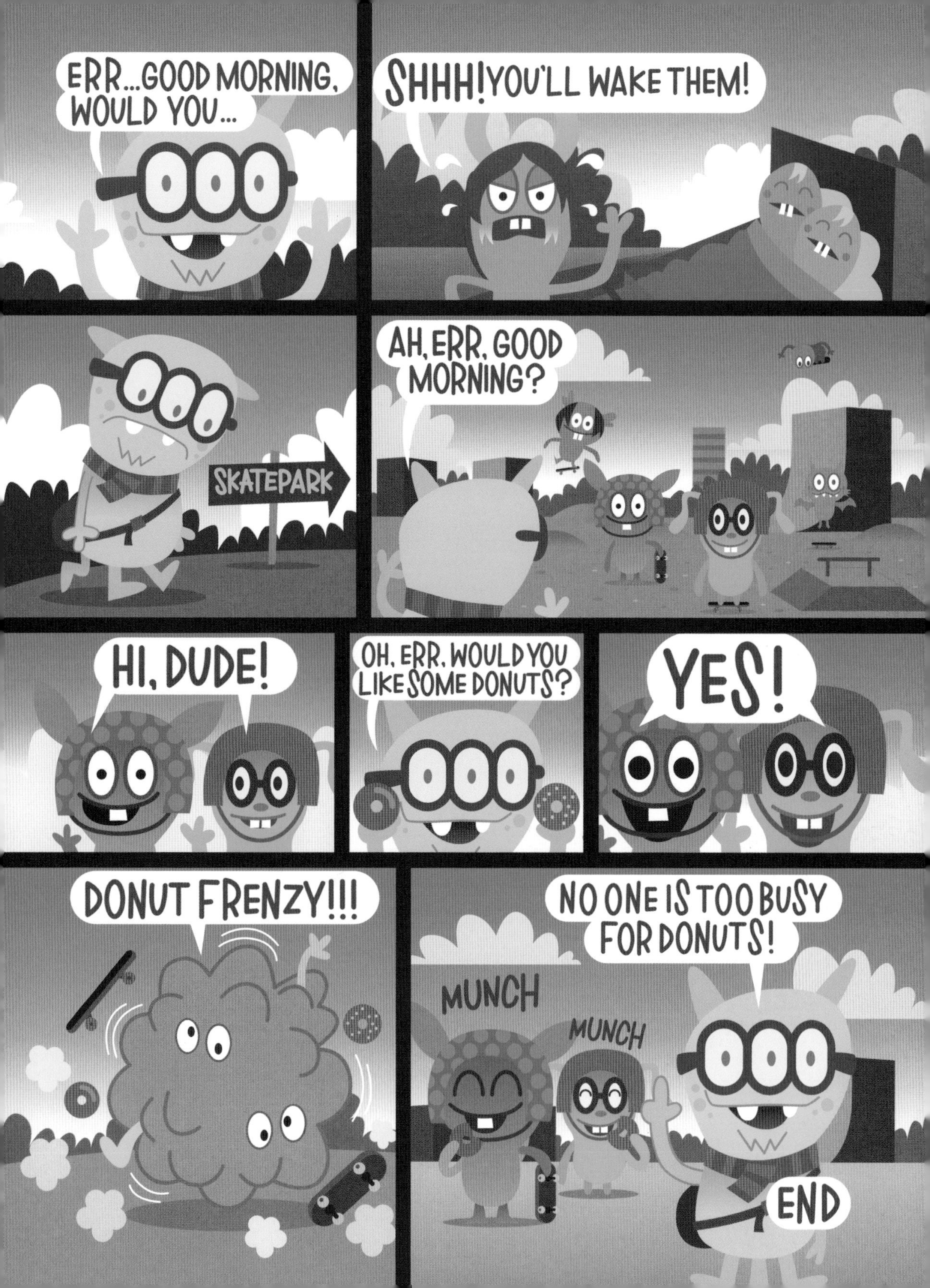
ERR...GOOD MORNING, WOULD YOU...
SHHH! YOU'LL WAKE THEM!
SKATEPARK
AH, ERR, GOOD MORNING?
HI, DUDE!
OH, ERR, WOULD YOU LIKE SOME DONUTS?
YES!
DONUT FRENZY!!!
NO ONE IS TOO BUSY FOR DONUTS!
MUNCH
MUNCH
END

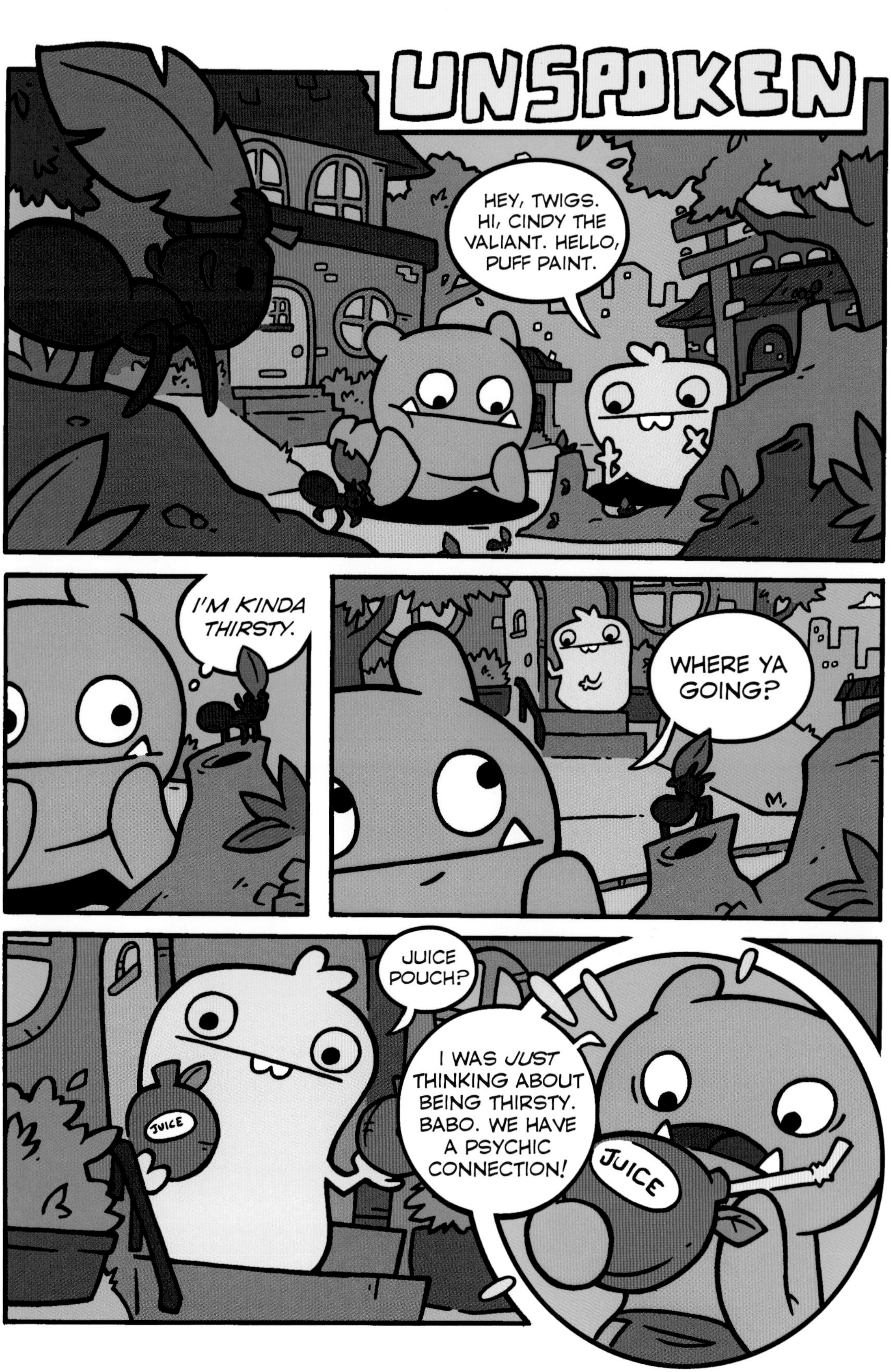
UNSPOKEN
HEY, TWIGS. HI, CINDY THE VALIANT. HELLO, PUFF PAINT.
I'M KINDA THIRSTY.
WHERE YA GOING?
JUICE POUCH?
I WAS JUST THINKING ABOUT BEING THIRSTY. BABO. WE HAVE A PSYCHIC CONNECTION!
JUICE
JUICE

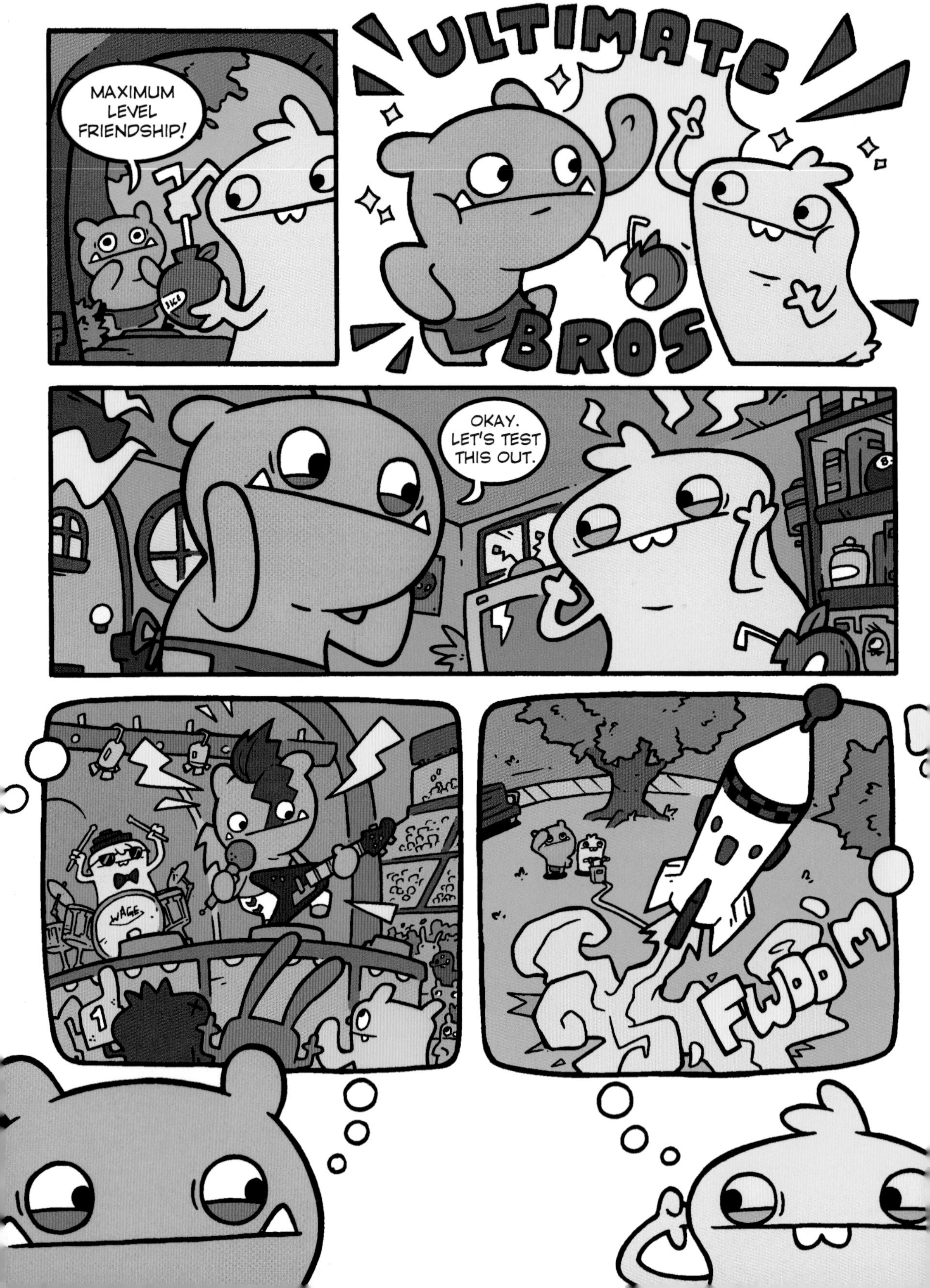
MAXIMUM LEVEL FRIENDSHIP!
ULTIMATE BROS
OKAY. LET'S TEST THIS OUT.
WAGE
FWOOM

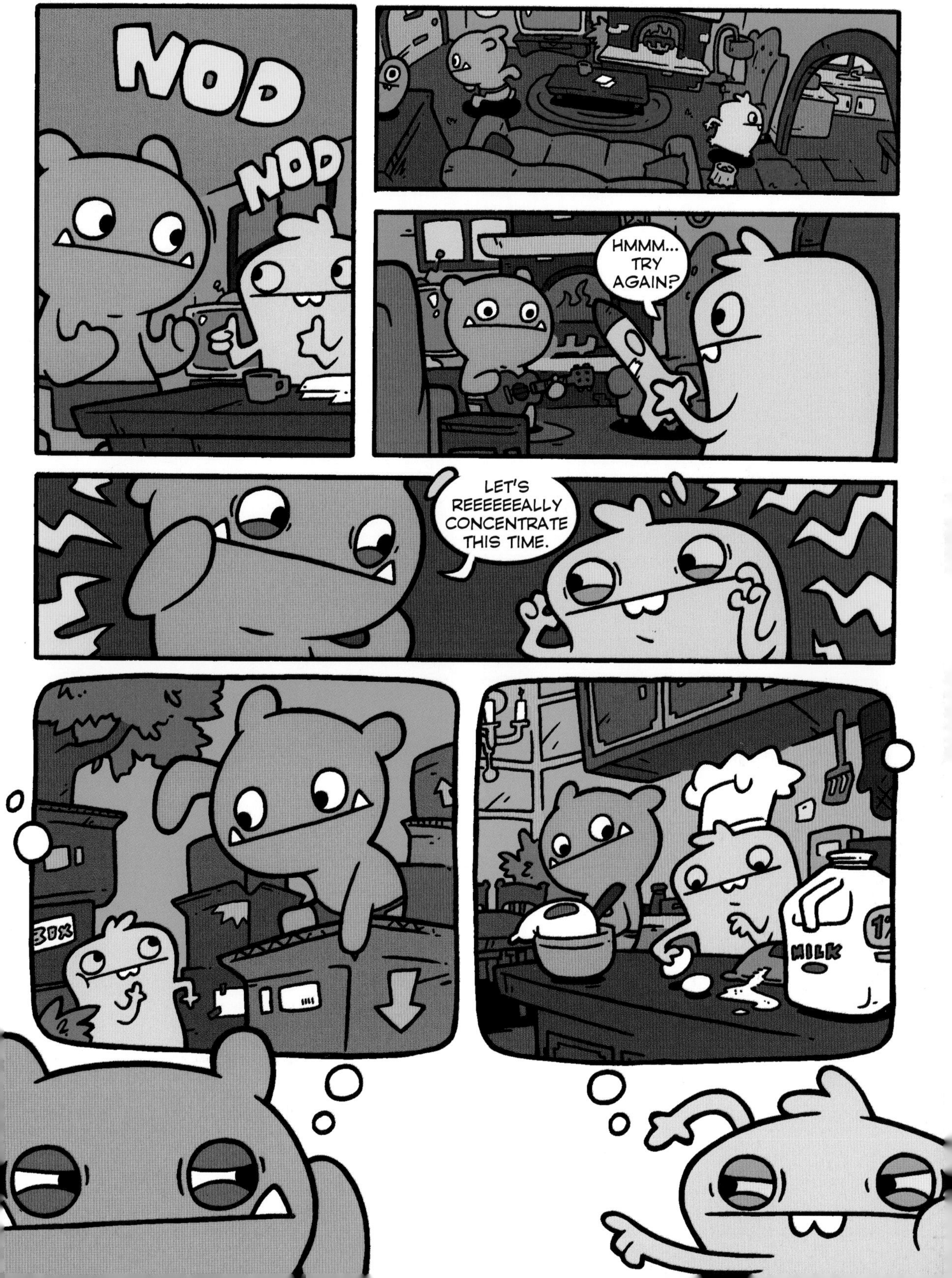
NOD
NOD
HMMM... TRY AGAIN?
LET'S REEEEEEEALLY CONCENTRATE THIS TIME.
MILK
1%

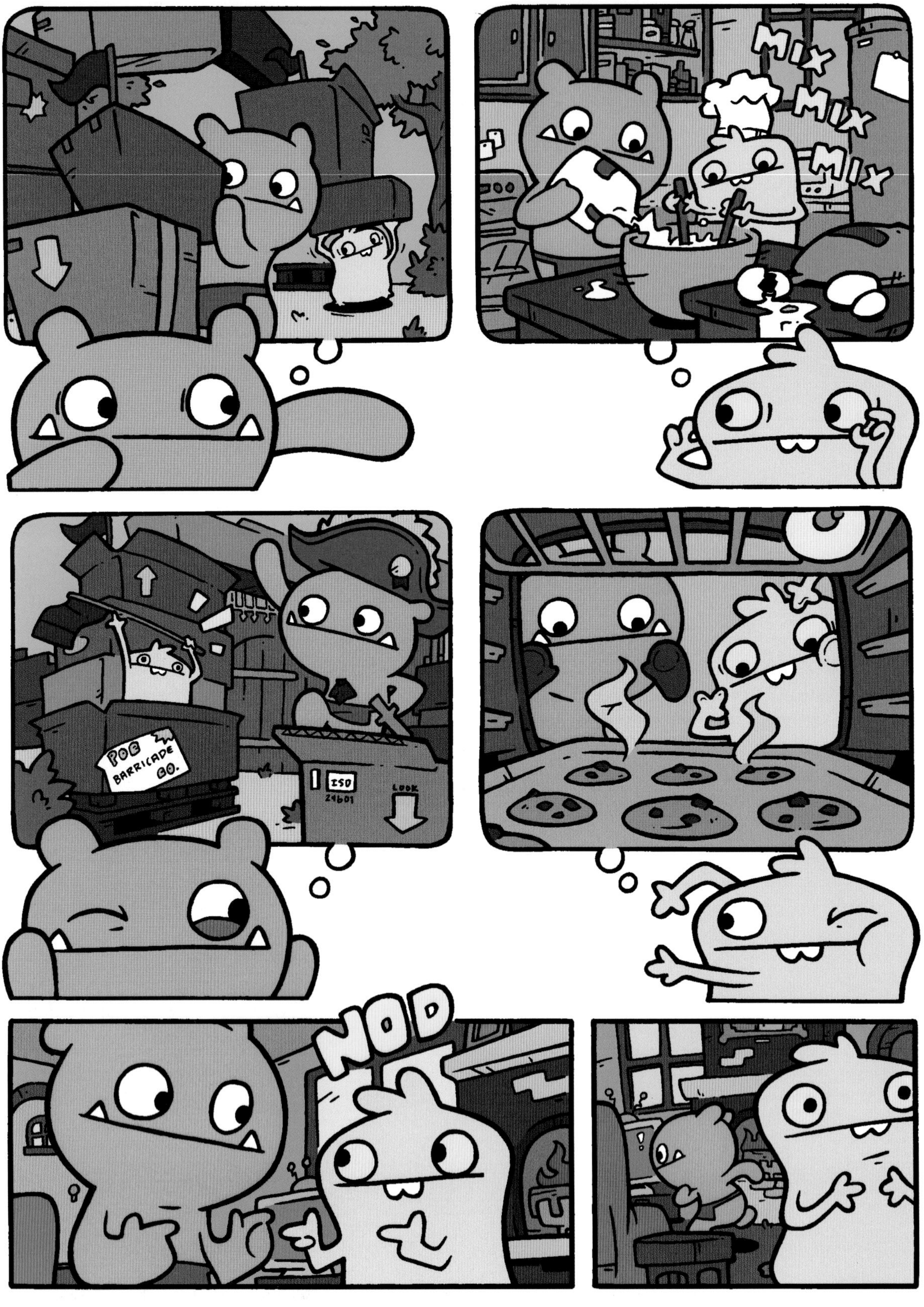
MIX
MIX
MIX
POE
BARRICADE
CO.
ISD
24601
LOOK
NOD

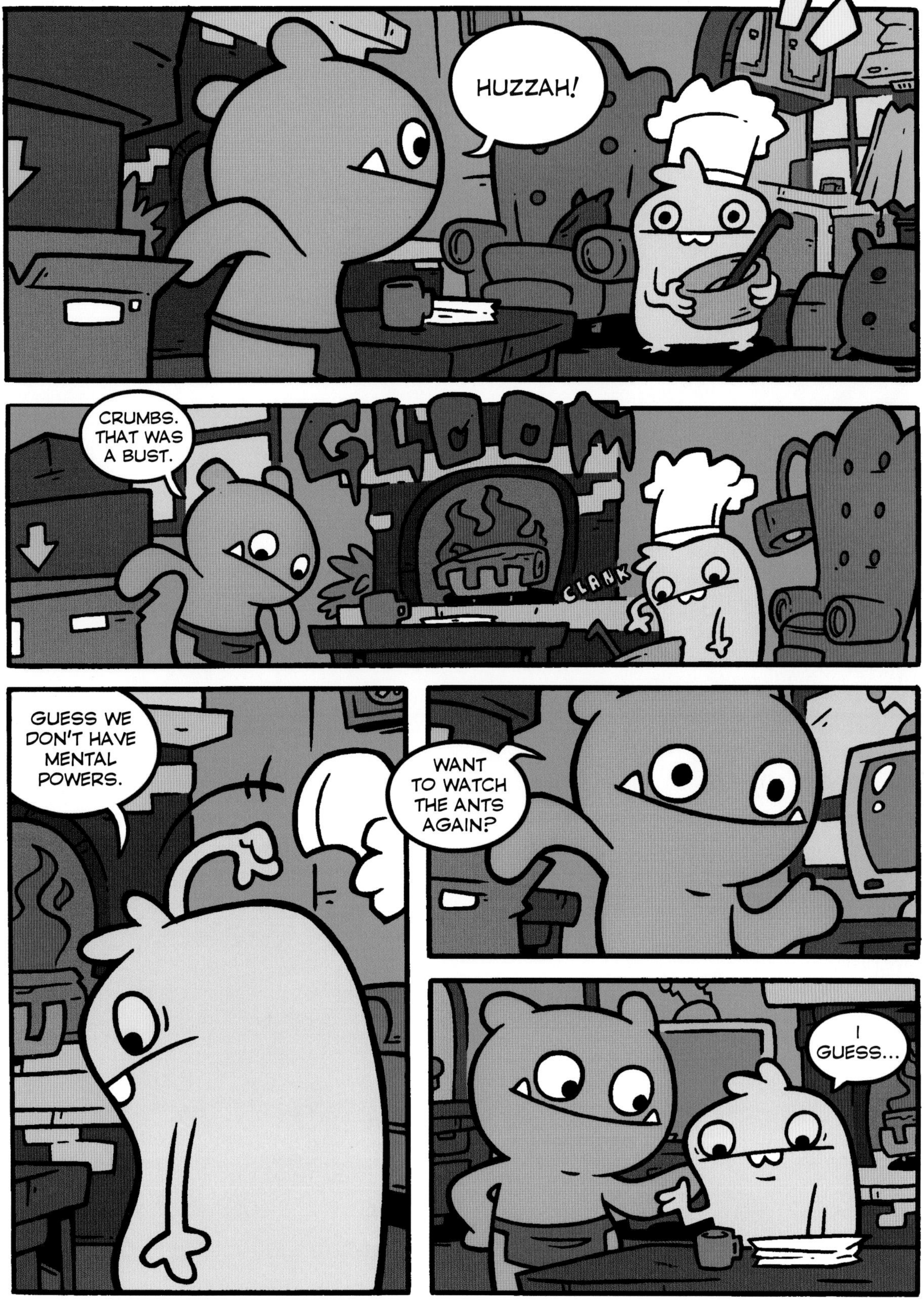
HUZZAH!
CRUMBS. THAT WAS A BUST.
GLOOM
CLANK
GUESS WE DON'T HAVE MENTAL POWERS.
WANT TO WATCH THE ANTS AGAIN?
I GUESS...

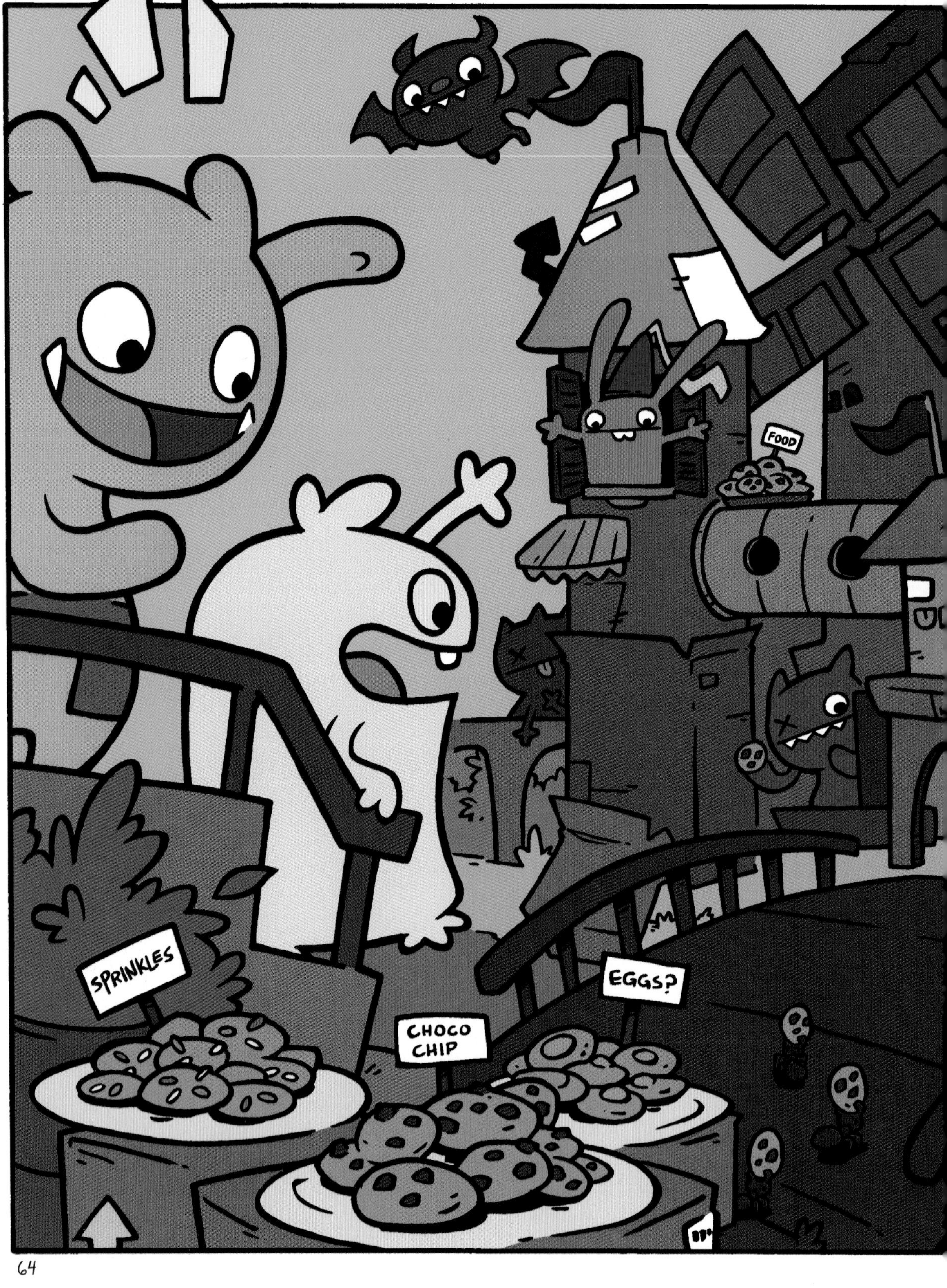
FOOD
SPRINKLES
CHOCO CHIP
EGGS?

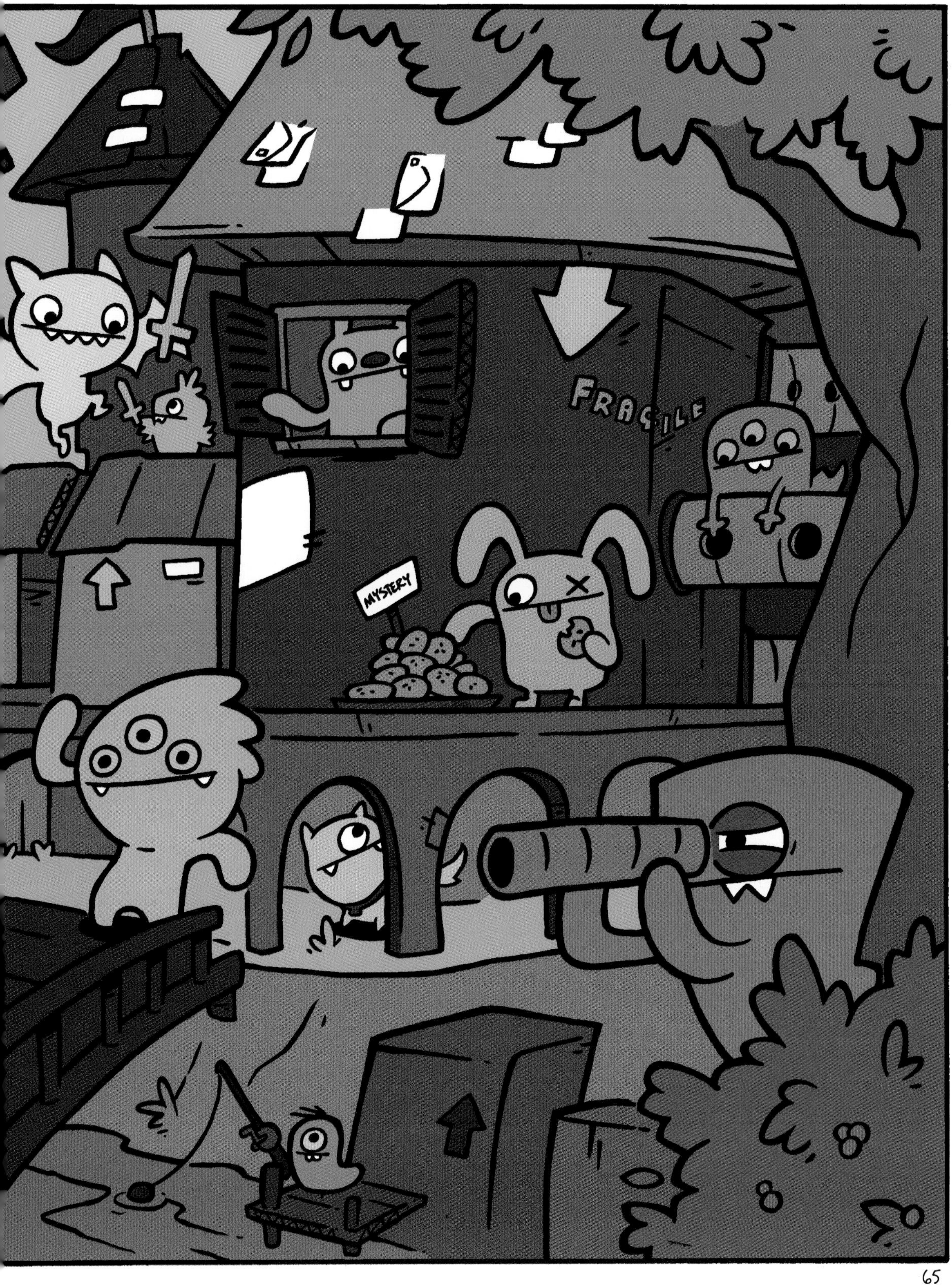
FRAGILE
MYSTERY

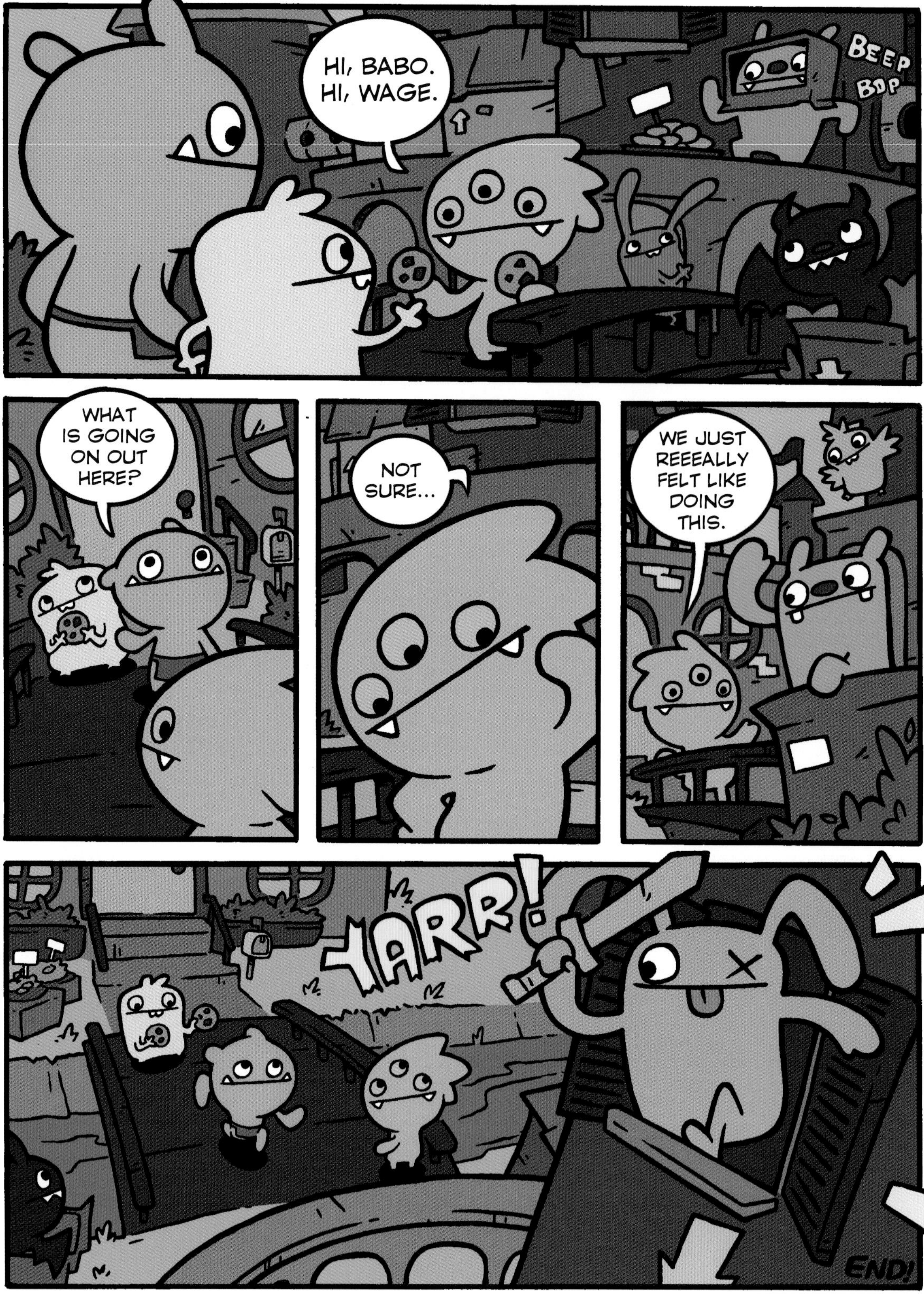
HI, BABO.
HI, WAGE.
BEEP
BOP
WHAT IS GOING ON OUT HERE?
NOT SURE...
WE JUST REEEALLY FELT LIKE DOING THIS.
YARR!
END!

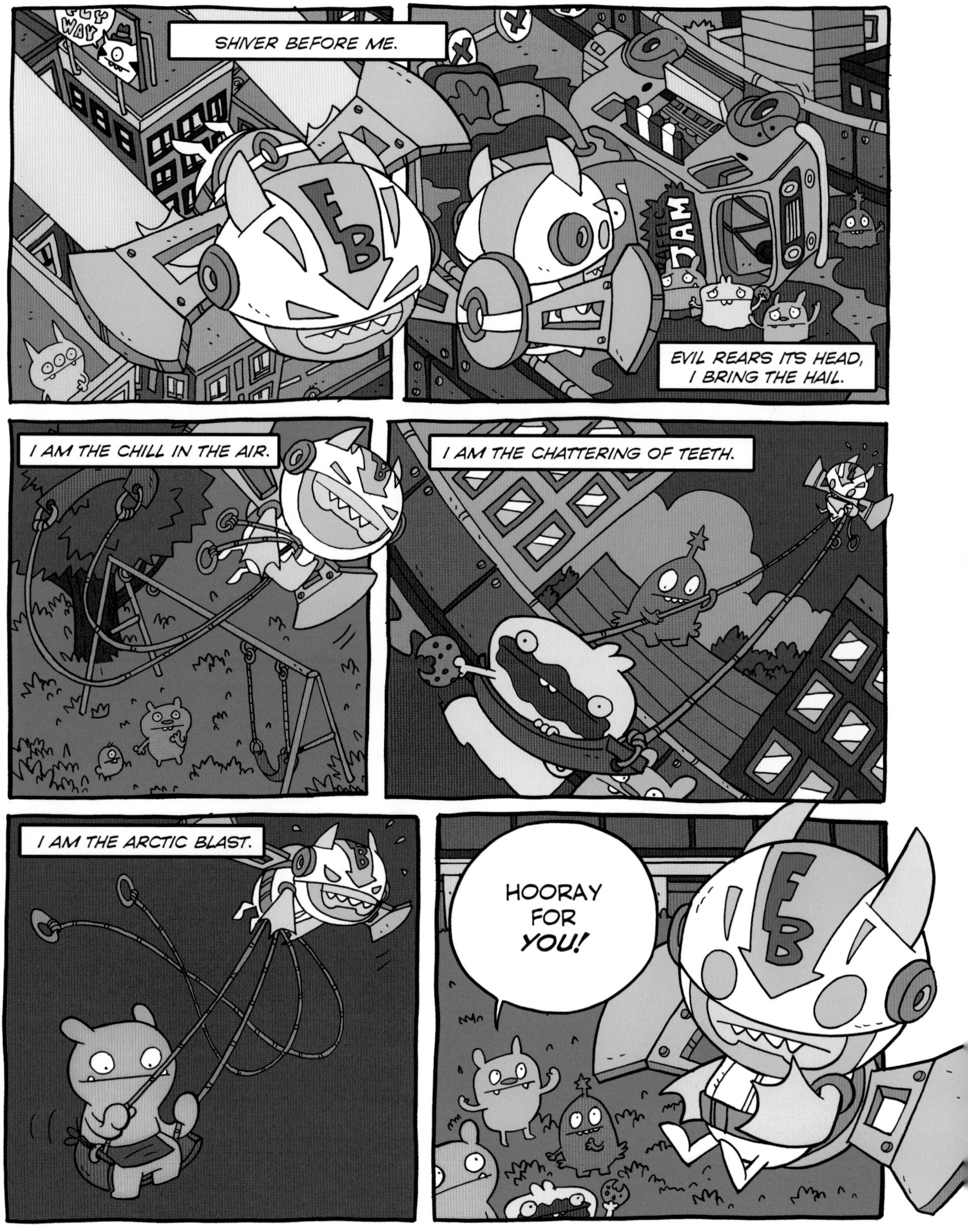

SHIVER BEFORE ME.
EVIL REARS ITS HEAD, I BRING THE HAIL.
I AM THE CHILL IN THE AIR.
I AM THE CHATTERING OF TEETH.
I AM THE ARCTIC BLAST.
HOORAY FOR *YOU!*

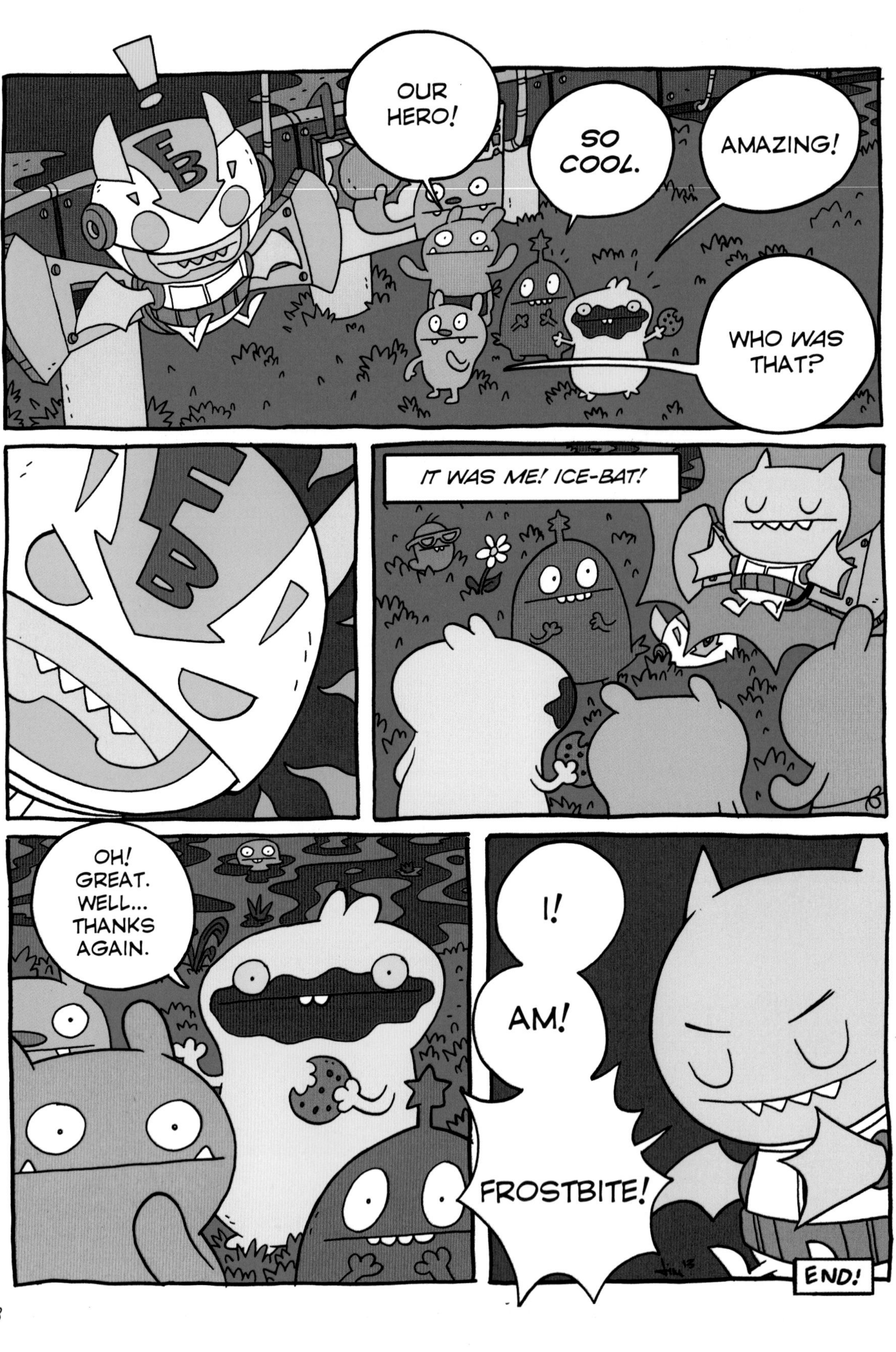
OUR HERO!
SO COOL.
AMAZING!
WHO WAS THAT?
IT WAS ME! ICE-BAT!
OH! GREAT. WELL... THANKS AGAIN.
I!
AM!
FROSTBITE!
END!

Good Morning!

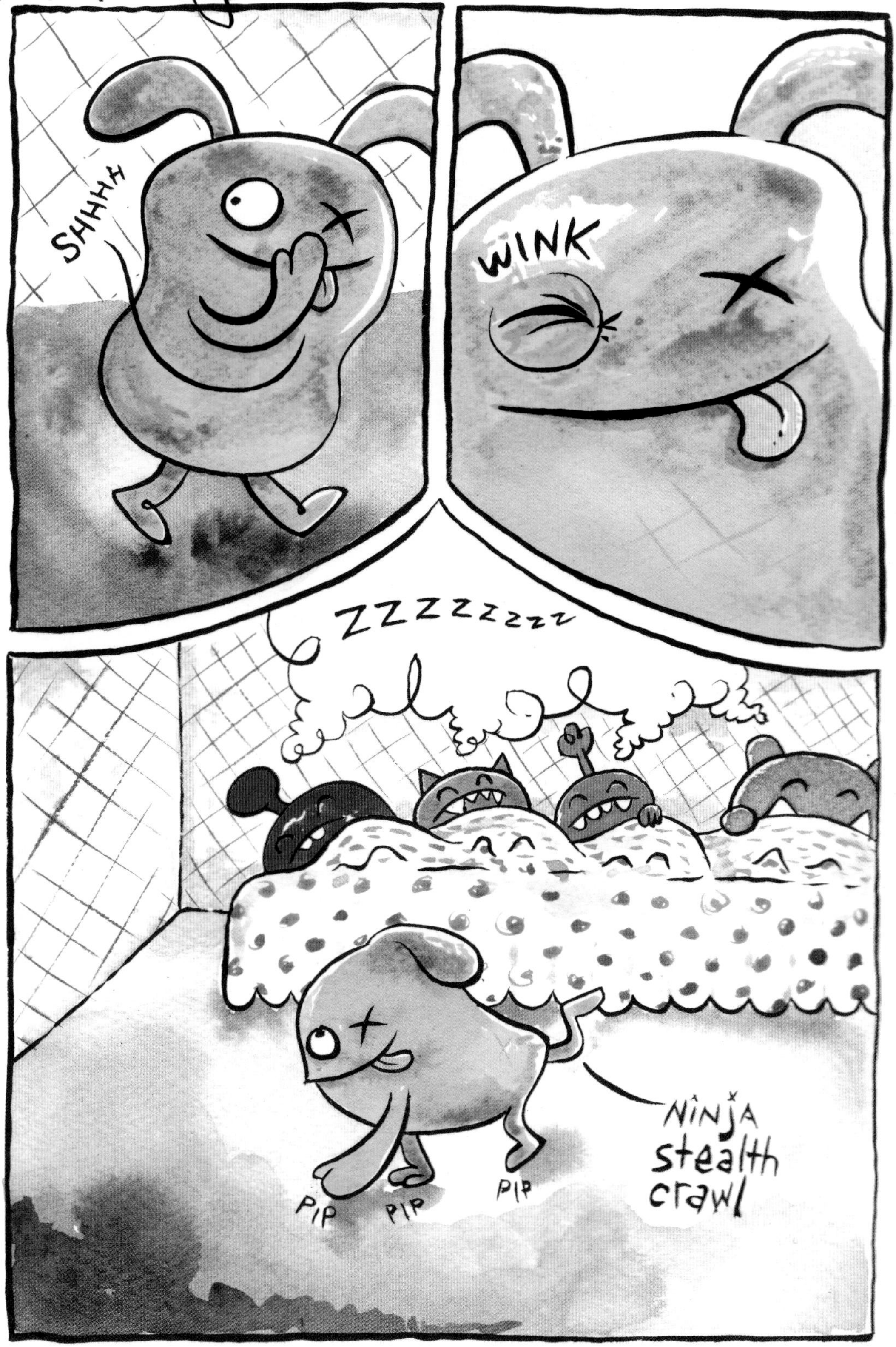
SHHHH
WINK
ZZZZZZzzz
NINJA stealth crawl
PIP
PIP
PIP

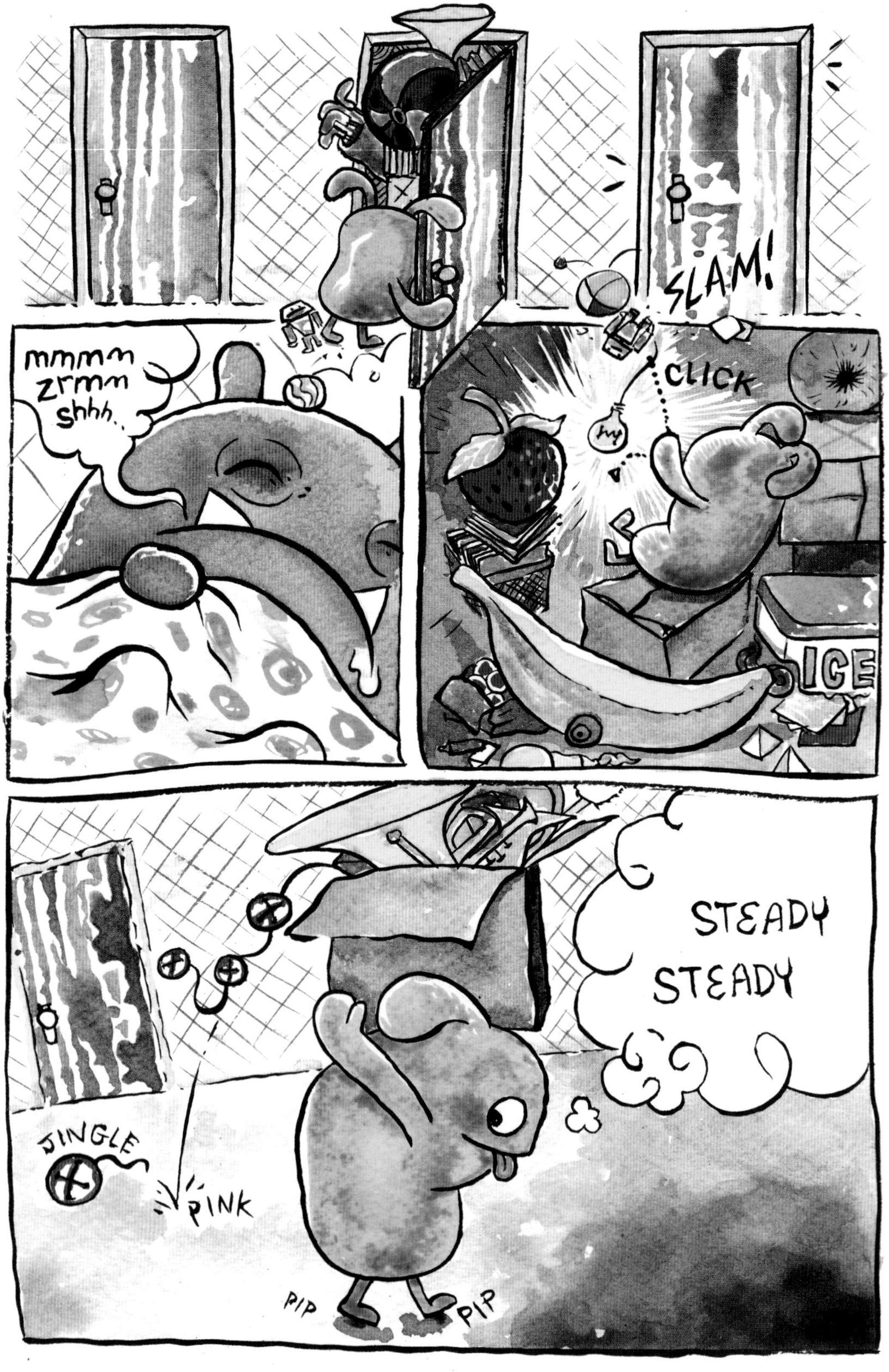
SLAM!
mmmm zrmm shhh...
CLICK
ICE
STEADY STEADY
JINGLE
PINK
PIP PIP

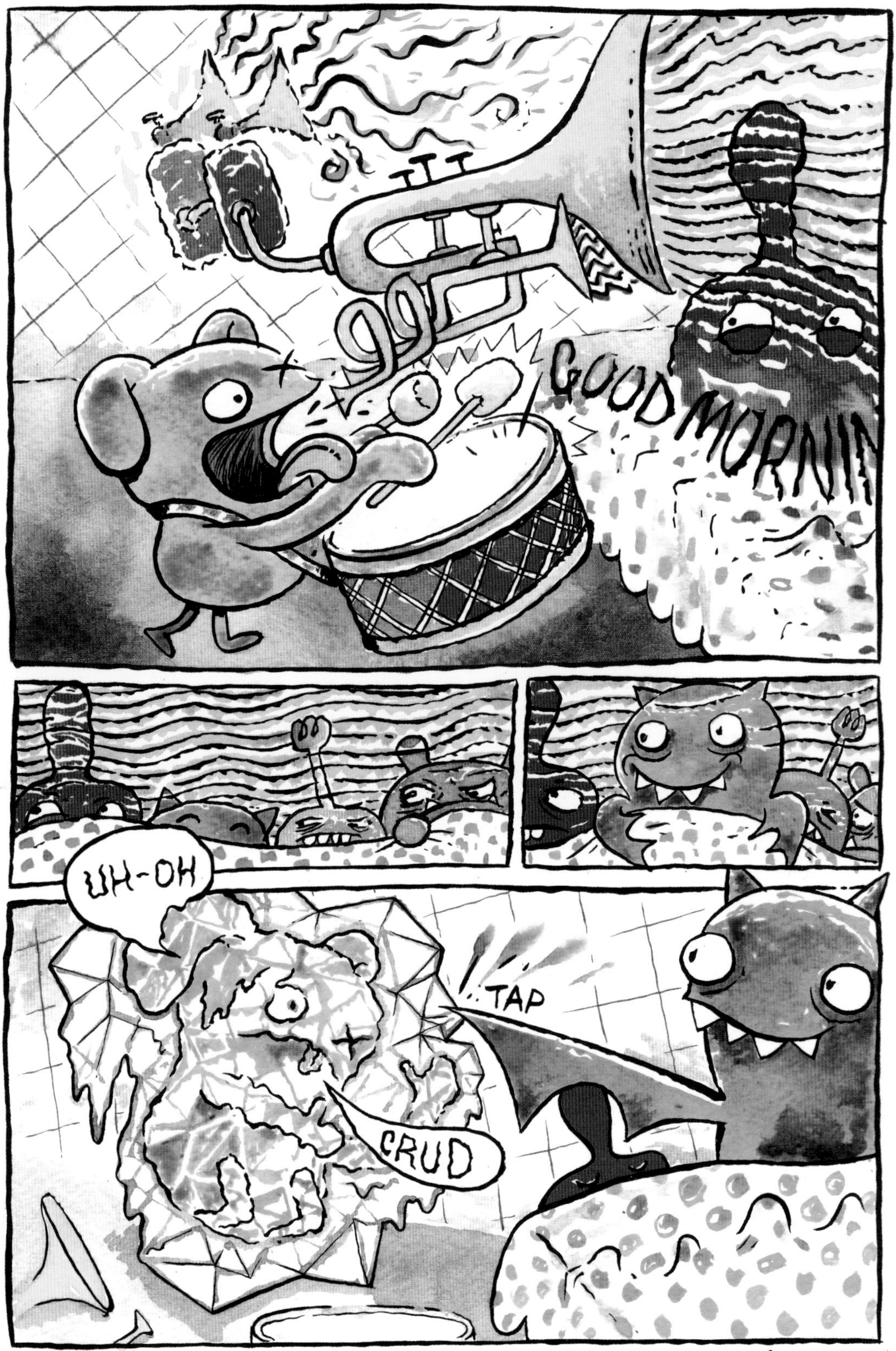
GOOD MORNIN
UH-OH
TAP
CRUD

The End

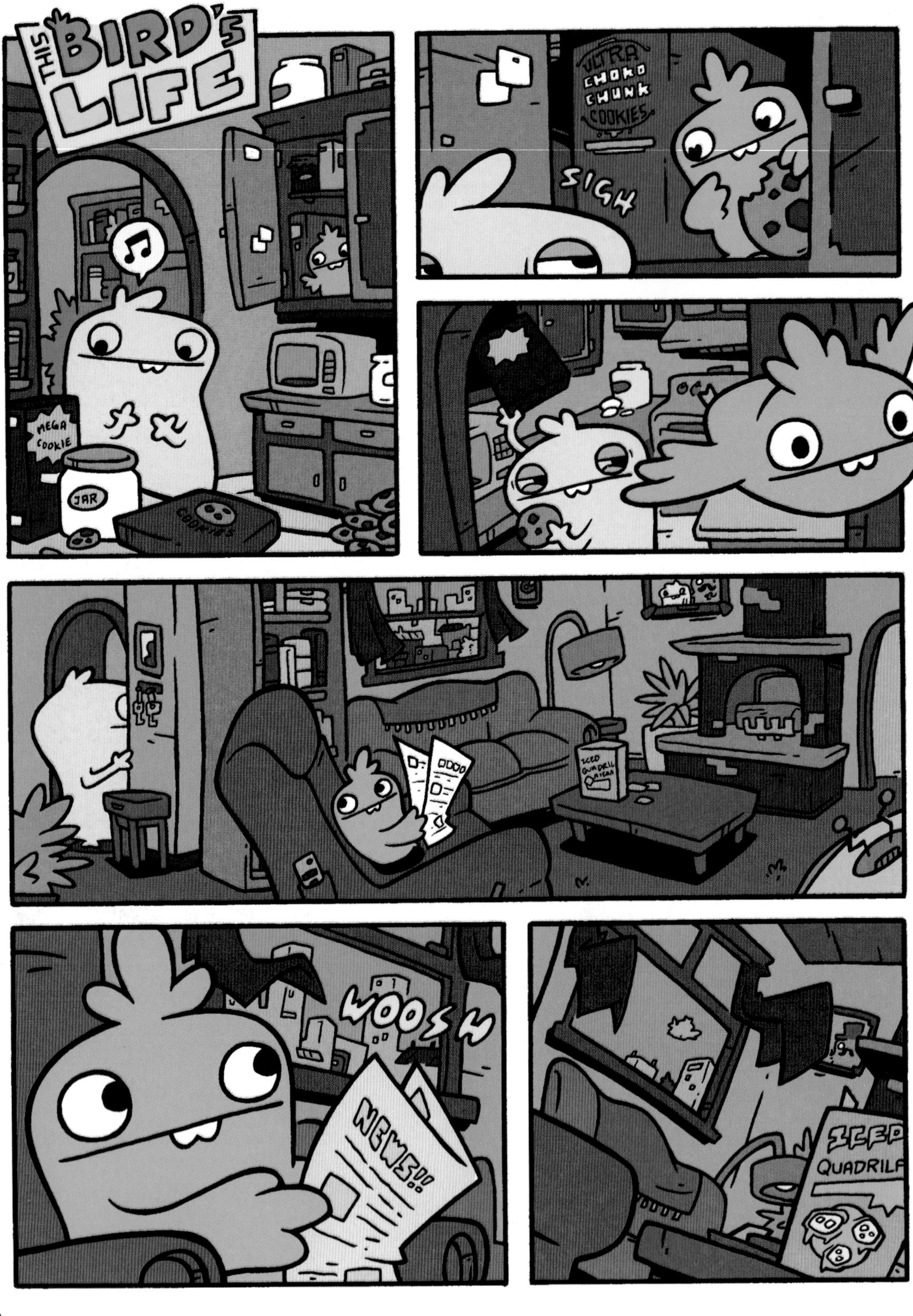
THE BIRD'S LIFE
MEGA COOKIE
JAR
COOKIES
ULTRA CHOKO CHUNK COOKIES
SIGH
WOOSH
NEWS!!
ICED
QUADRILA

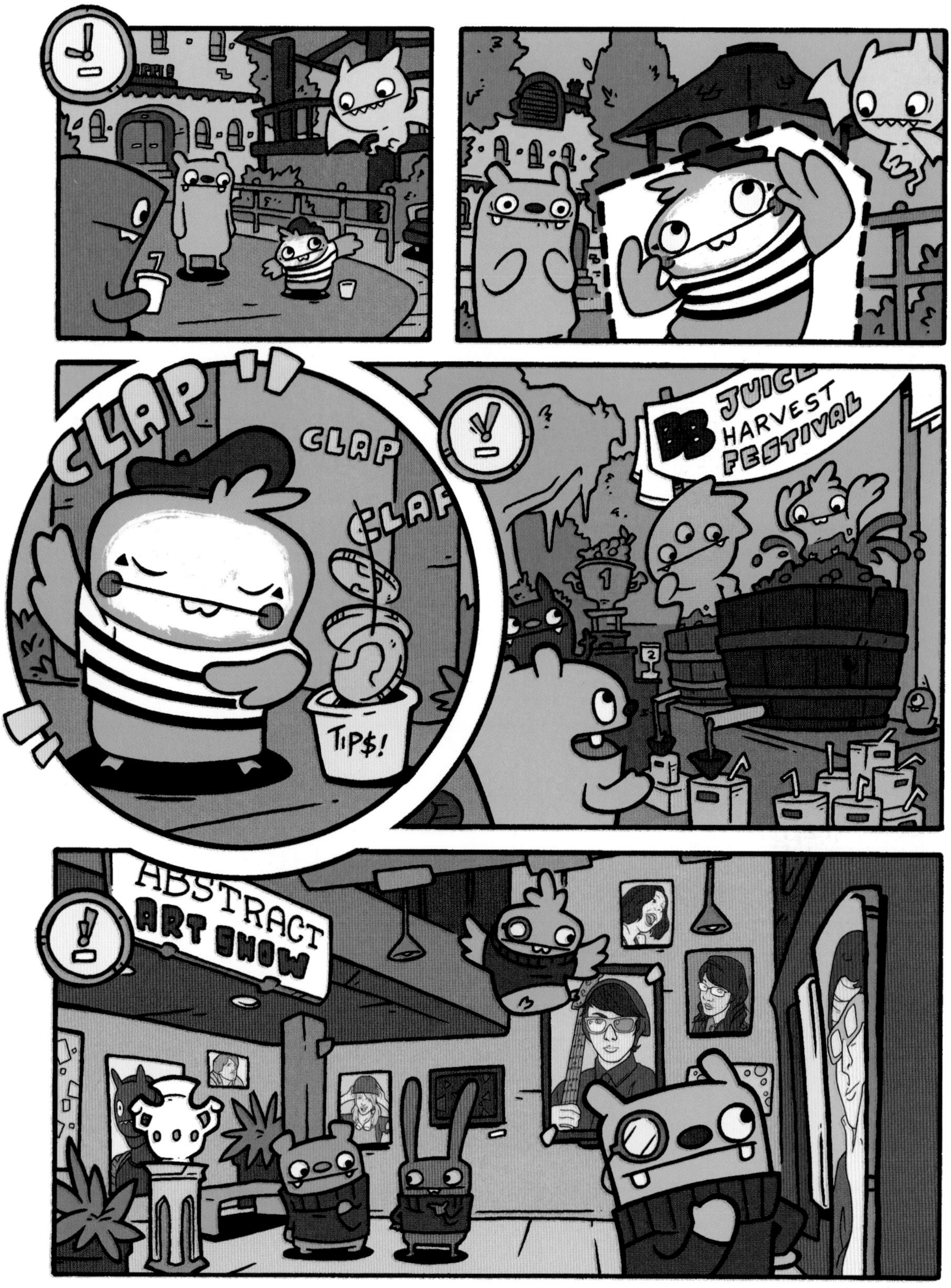
CLAP
CLAP
CLAP
TIP$!
BB JUICE HARVEST FESTIVAL
ABSTRACT ART SHOW

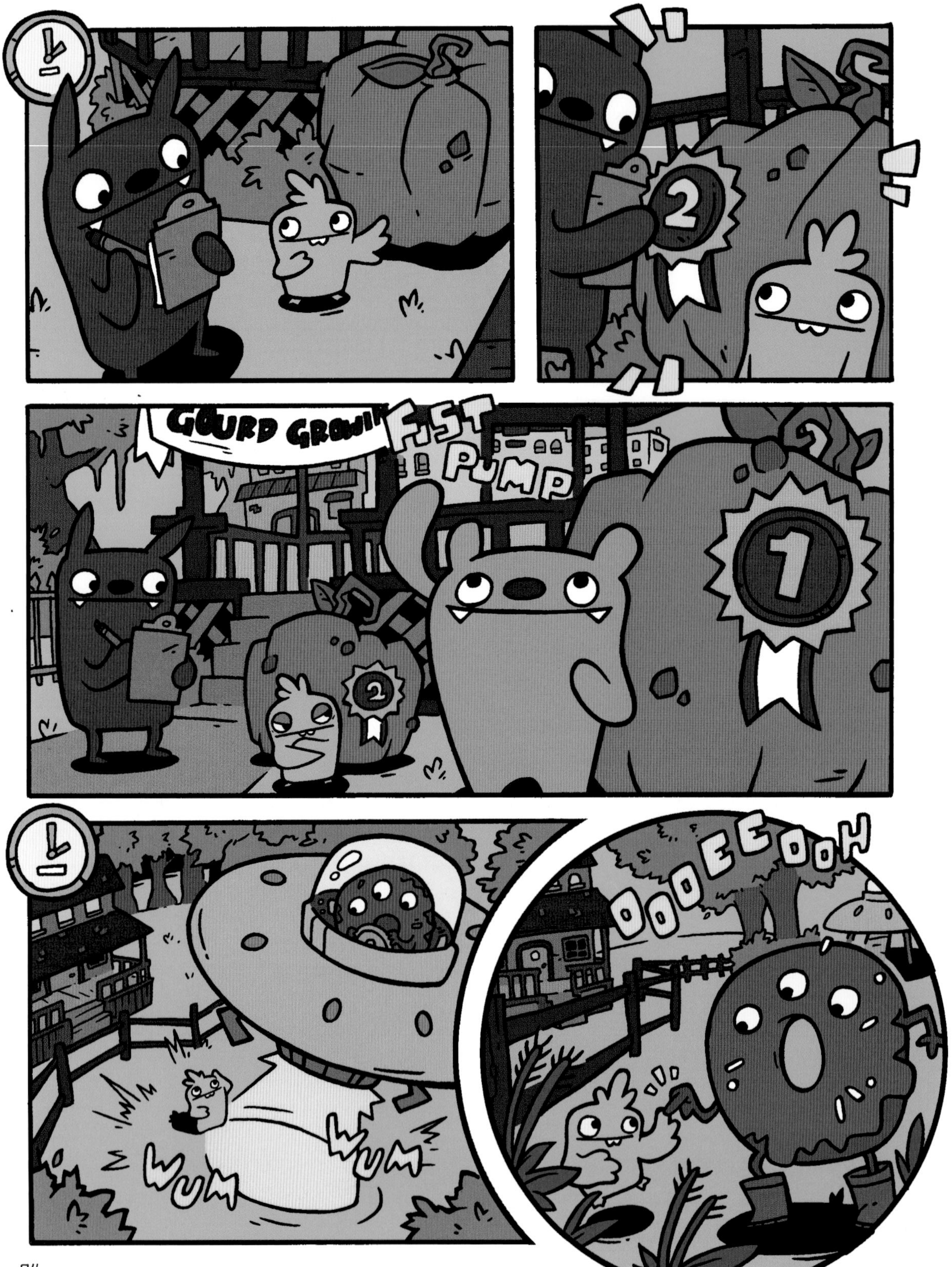
GOURD GROWI
FIST PUMP
WUM WUM
OOOEEOOH

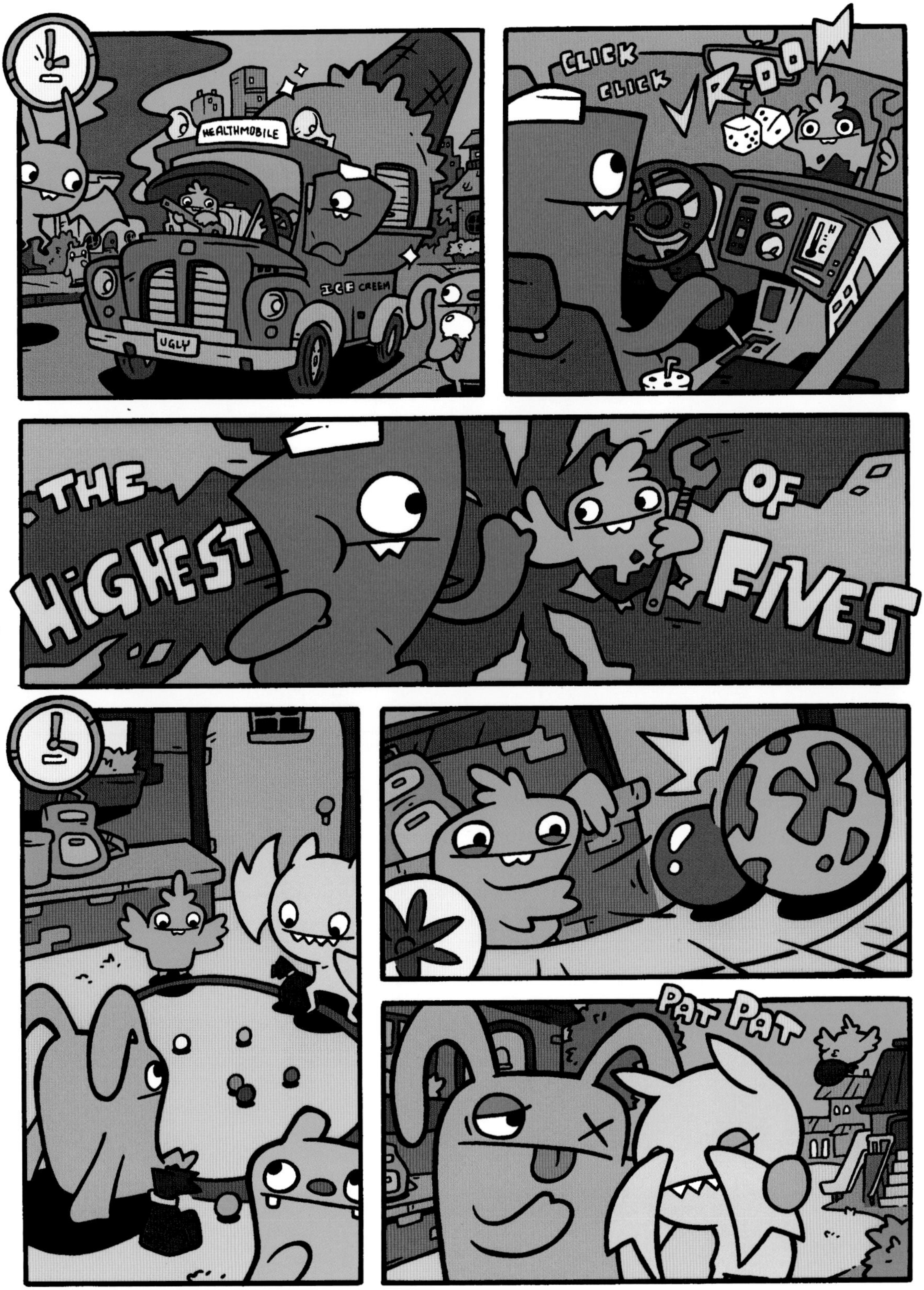
HEALTHMOBILE
ICE CREEM
UGLY
CLICK
CLICK
VROOM
THE HIGHEST OF FIVES
PAT PAT

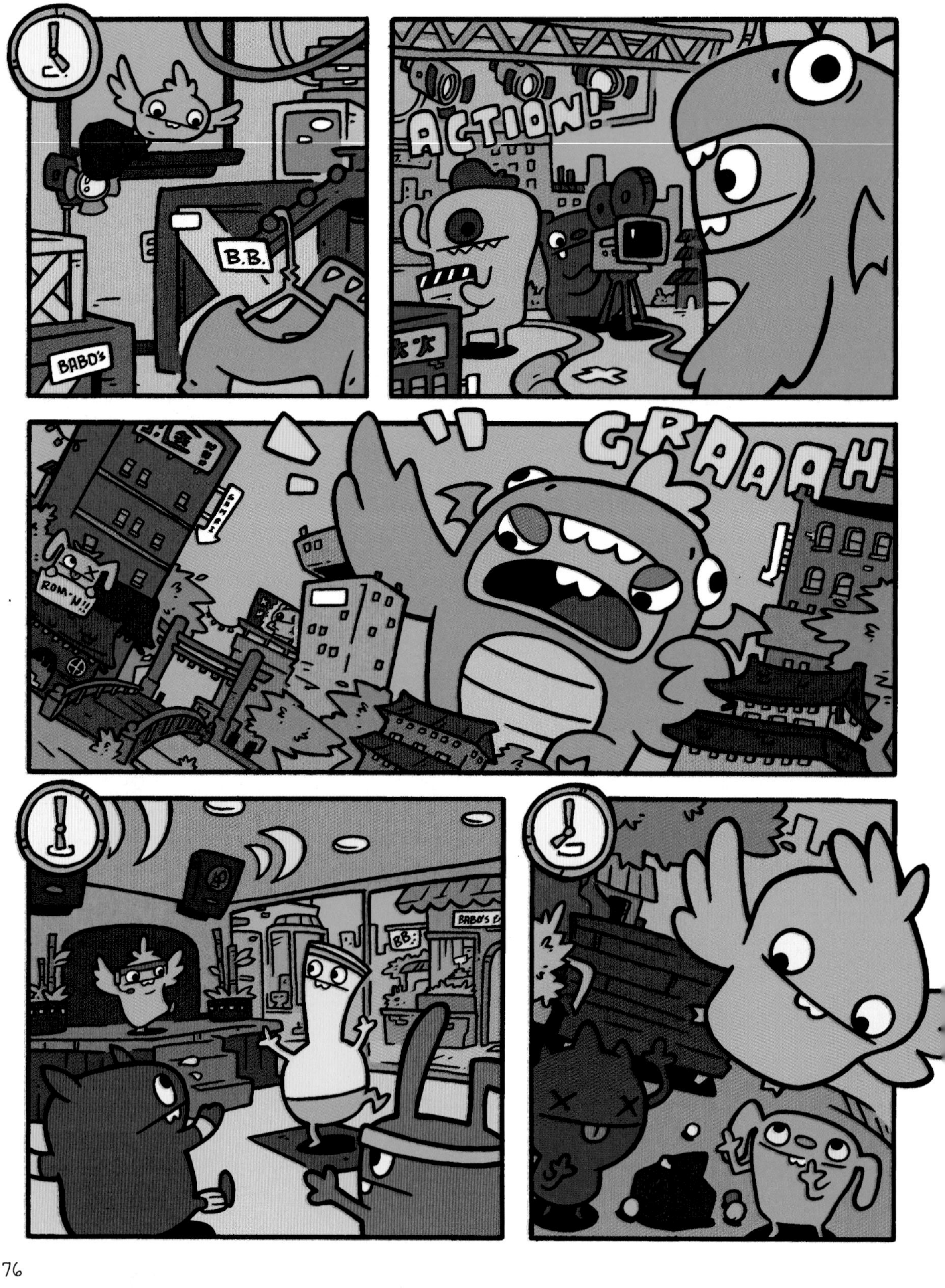

B.B.
BABO's
ACTION!
GRAAAH
ROM·N!!
BABO'S
B.B.

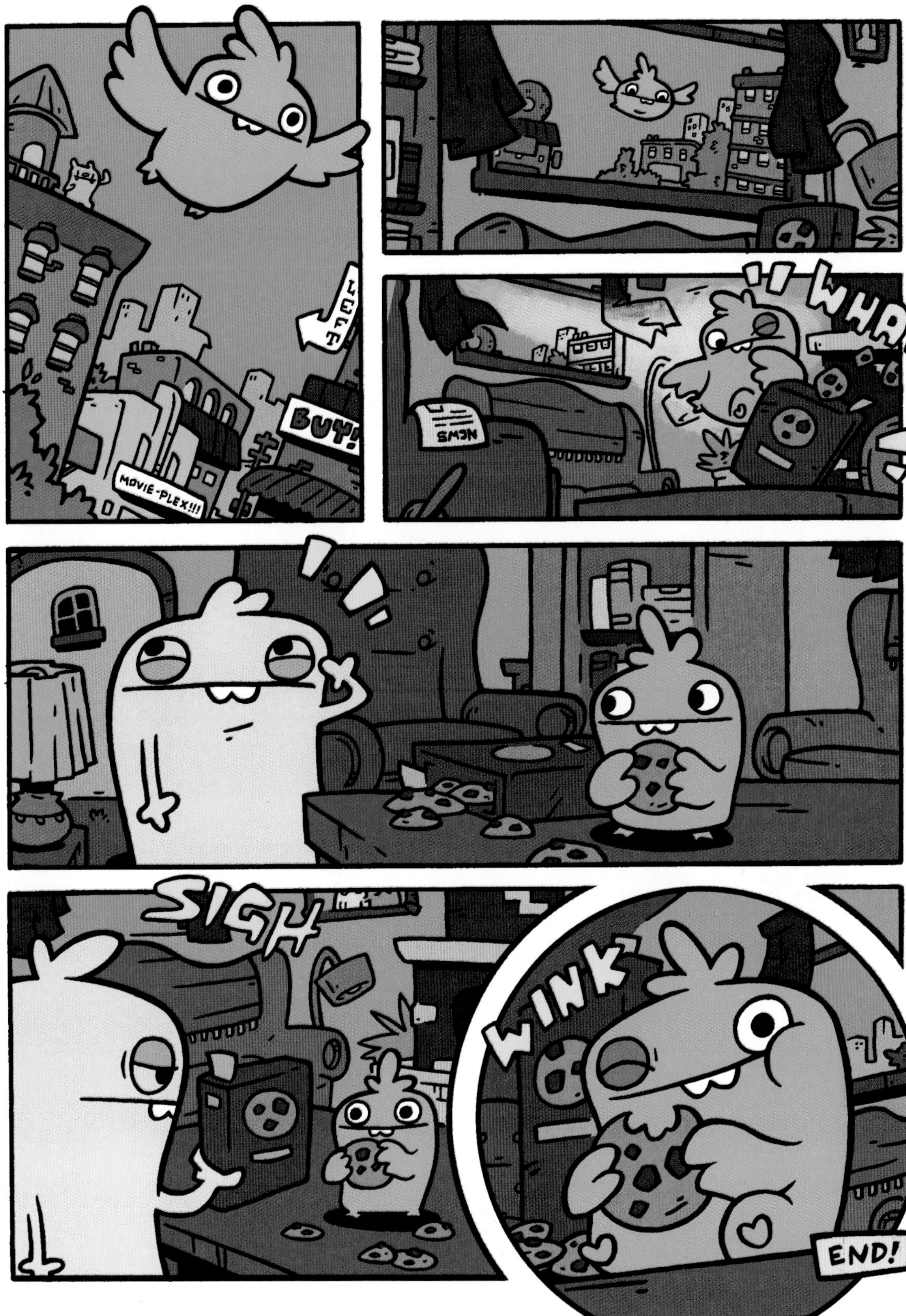
LEFT
BUY!
MOVIE-PLEX!!!
WHAP
SIGH
WINK
END!

BROUGHT

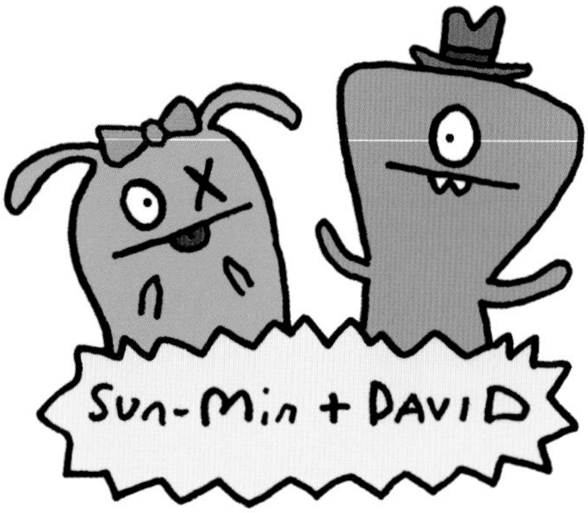
Sun-Min + DAVID

SUN-MIN KIM & DAVID HORVATH

are best known for creating the world of Uglydoll, which started as a line of handmade plush dolls and has since grown into a brand loved by all ages around the world. Their works can be found everywhere from the Moma in Tokyo and the Louvre in Paris, to the windows of their very own Uglydoll shop in Seoul. Sun-Min and David's very first conversation was about the meaning of "ugly." To them, ugly means unique and different, that which makes us who we are. It should never be hidden, but shouted from the rooftops! They wanted to build a world that showed the twists and turns that make us who we are, inside and out, because the whole world benefits when we embrace our true, twisty-turny selves. So, ugly is the new beauty. This Uglydoll comic features some of Sun-Min and David's heroes from the pop art and comic art world.

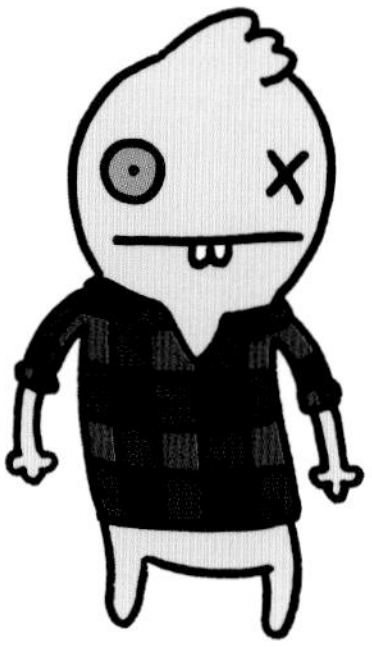

TRAVIS NICHOLS

is the author and illustrator of several books for kids and post-kids, including *The Monster Doodle Book*, *Punk Rock Etiquette* and *Matthew Meets the Man*. He previously drew comics for the late, great *Nickelodeon Magazine*. His deepest, most secret wish is to wake up as a gnome and spend his days building wooden locks, eating tiny biscuits and hanging out with birds. He can be found eating watermelon over the sink or online.

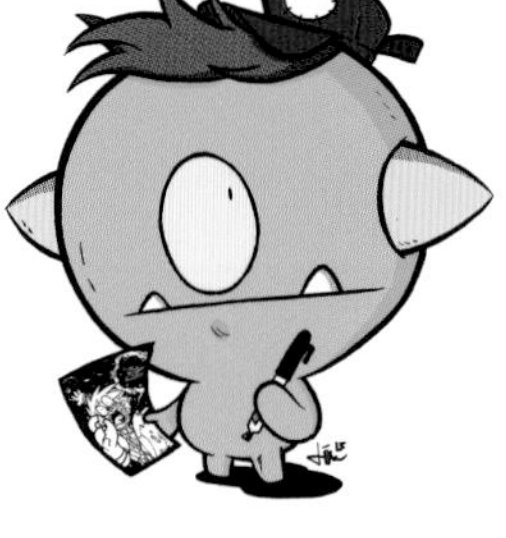

IAN MCGINTY

is a real smiley dude! And he wants to know where you got that cool lunchbox! You know, the one with the dinosaur riding a great white shark?
Oh, is this Gilbert Johnson? No? Gosh, sorry for bothering you! Um...okay, bye.

PHILLIP JACOBSON

is a 23-year-old graduate student at the Savannah College of Art and Design studying sequential art. His earlier works include the self-published titles *Battle Mammals* and *Pancakes for Yeti*. Some of his influences include Bryan Lee O'Malley, Madeline Rupert and Craig Bartlett. He would like to thank his late grandmother Mary Ann Hill for constantly encouraging him to draw when he was little and for inspiring him to pursue his artistic goals.

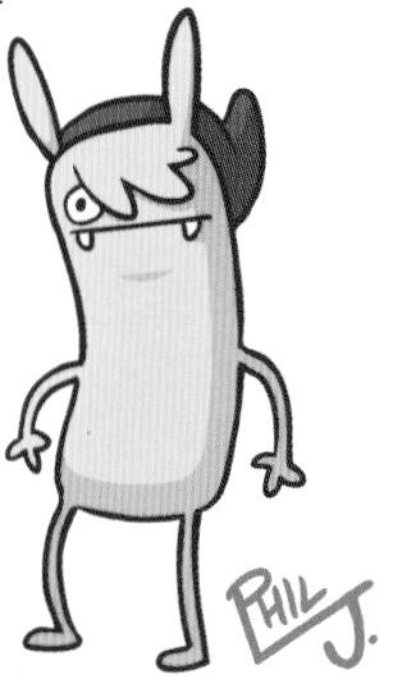
PHIL J.

TO YOU BY:

CHANMEN

独自の視点で玩具を中心に深く創作活動を続けるクリエイター集団『GARGAMEL』所属のアーティスト。
A member of the Gargemel artist group, Chanmen profoundly believes that toys are at the heart of his creative endeavors.

グラフィック、キャラクター、カスタムペイントからパッケージまで、目につく場所の全てデザインする。
From graphic design to character design, from custom paint-work to packaging, Chanmen does it all.

幼少期から続けられる膨大な玩具・小物・書籍のコレクションから得られた莫大な知識とセンスは、『イラストレーター』としてのCHANMENが最大級に活かされている。
Since childhood, Chanmen has been influenced by large scale toys, small accessories and books, developing his sense of style as an illustrator.

その才能は国内外でのART SHOWへコンスタントな出展に注入され、世界のTOYコレクター、ARTコレクター達の心を時めかす存在となっている。
His talent is regularly on display at art shows, making the hearts of toy and art collectors around the world beat faster.

PETE FOWLER's

art roams the fields of music, illustration, toy design, printmaking, painting, commercial clients and more recently, cross-stitch embroidery. Some of his most recognizable images include designs for Super Furry Animals' albums, videos, merchandise and giant inflatable bears. His Monsterism creations have gained a worldwide fan base.
Pete is also one half of the cosmic smooth rock/deckshoe gaze music duo Seahawks, releasing music prolifically since 2010.

Hi, my name is ## BWANA SPOONS.

I am a painter and half jack of many other trades. I heart trees, moss and monsters. I make toys and design shoes and bust out the occasional illustration. I make art. I also own and run Grass Hut Art Market, a gallery and retail space based in Portland, Oregon.
I have shown my arts in various corners of the earth including Paris, Tokyo, San Francisco and Los Angeles. Most recently I worked on a few large murals and installations in Los Angeles and Tokyo. That was fun.

MICHAEL E. WIGGAM

is a professional comic book colorist whose work includes *Voltron Force* for VIZ Media, *Star Wars: Clone Wars* for Dark Horse Comics, *Raymond E. Feist's Magician Master: Enter the Great One* for Marvel Comics, *R.P.M.* and *I.C.E.* for 12 Gauge Comics, and various other publications. He was born and raised in Florida but has lived in Europe and seven U.S. states. Currently, he is earning an MFA from Savannah College of Art and Design.

SHHHHHHHHHHHHHHHH